Devine's Mission

When Lachlan McKinley raids Fairmount Town's bank, the four-thousand-dollar bounty that is posted on his head attracts plenty of manhunters, but everyone that goes after him ends up dead.

Bounty hunter Jonathon Lynch reckons he could do better. Lachlan is Jonathon's stepbrother and his mission is personal, but when he joins the hunt he soon discovers that all is not as it seems and Lachlan may, in fact, be innocent. Worse, US Marshal Jake Devine is also after Lachlan.

Devine is more likely to destroy the peace than to keep it, and so can Jonathon bring the guilty to justice before Devine does his worst?

Devine's Mission

I.J. Parnham

A Black Horse Western

ROBERT HALE

© I.J. Parnham 2017
First published in Great Britain 2017

ISBN 978-0-7198-2155-4

The Crowood Press
The Stable Block
Crowood Lane
Ramsbury
Marlborough
Wiltshire SN8 2HR

www.bhwesterns.com

Robert Hale is an imprint
of The Crowood Press

The right of I.J. Parnham to be identified as
author of this work has been asserted by him
in accordance with the Copyright, Designs and
Patents Act 1988

Typeset by
Derek Doyle & Associates, Shaw Heath
Printed and bound in Great Britain by
CPI Group (UK) Ltd, Croydon, CR0 4YY

CHAPTER 1

'If I'd have known you'd be here, I wouldn't have come to Bear Creek,' Jonathon Lynch said.

Willoughby Jeffries snorted a laugh. 'You're not the first one to say that tonight.'

Willoughby gestured to the corner of the Long Trail saloon where three other men had gathered at a table. Jonathon recognized only one of them, Cameron Morgan, his long-time rival and the man who had invited him here.

While Cameron appraised Jonathon with a lively gleam in his eye, Willoughby identified the other two men as being Broderick Trent and Reinhart Vane. The names meant nothing to Jonathon, but he recognized the type.

He joined Willoughby in heading to the table where he picked up the only spare glass and leaned back in his chair. He glanced around the otherwise deserted room before facing Cameron.

'Only one unused glass,' he said. 'Does that mean I'm the last to arrive?'

'It does,' Cameron said. 'And so now we can talk business.'

While the other men murmured sighs of relief, Jonathon poured himself a large measure of whiskey.

'It's about time,' Broderick said.

'This had better be worth my time,' Reinhart said.

'It will be,' Cameron said. He withdrew a folded-up 'Wanted' poster from his pocket and spread it out on the table.

The other four men leaned forward to read the details. It depicted the square-jawed face of an individual identified as being Lachlan McKinley, who was wanted for raiding the bank in Fairmount Town.

The name made Jonathon flinch, but he didn't detect that anyone noticed his discomfort; they were all busy showing their surprise at the level of bounty on offer for Lachlan's capture – four thousand dollars.

'That's a mighty tempting offer,' Jonathon said. 'So why are you sitting here drinking with us instead of going after him?'

'I first came across this poster six months ago in a saloon not unlike this one,' Cameron said. 'And I listened to a group of four bounty hunters not unlike this group discuss which one of them would collect.'

'As you're showing us this poster, I'd guess that the answer is none of them.'

'You guessed right. Then again, I'm the only one out of the original group who can collect. The others have all gone missing and it's likely they're now dead.'

Jonathon swirled his drink and then placed the glass down on the table.

'Which must mean they got close to Lachlan while you didn't.'

Cameron picked up his glass and sipped his drink.

'It doesn't. I'm here to tell you this tale because I decided not to go after Lachlan. Something was just plain wrong about the situation. For a start, have any of you seen the bank in Fairmount Town?'

'I once passed through the town,' Willoughby said. 'It was large and prosperous, but I don't remember seeing the bank.'

'Exactly,' Cameron said with a smile. 'Fairmount Town's bank is so small I doubt it's ever had four thousand dollars in it, which means someone's posted a massive bounty to bring in a man for what looks like a minor crime. That sounded mighty odd to me and I didn't want to waste my time finding out what was going on.'

'Until now?' Jonathon asked.

'Let's just say that when Miguel Castillo, a man who always finds his quarry, went missing, I got intrigued. So I decided to gather together the best bounty hunters in the business to discuss the situation.' Cameron knocked back his drink. 'Unfortunately, they weren't interested and so I called for you people instead.'

Everyone laughed. Then, with the purpose of this meeting detailed, Cameron said no more, leaving the others to glance at each other. Willoughby was the first to respond.

'If you're hoping the five of us will band together to find Lachlan, you'll be disappointed,' he said. 'I work alone.'

Broderick and Reinhart both murmured that this applied to them, too.

'I wasn't suggesting that,' Cameron said. 'While I'm busy risking my life, I don't want to get double-crossed by any of you folk.'

Willoughby conceded the slur with a shrug. 'So what are you suggesting?'

'It looks as if four bounty hunters have died trying to find Lachlan. If you decide to go after him, unless we help each other you'll probably suffer the same fate, so I reckon we should agree to share information and not to hinder each other.'

Willoughby licked his lips and then rocked his

head from side to side as he considered his response.

'That would suggest we need to be careful, not that we should collude.'

'That's one way of looking at it, but I'm hoping we can do better, and I'm prepared to be the first to offer something useful. Everyone that died headed to Fairmount Town to check out the details about the bank raid, but after they left the town, none of them was ever seen again.' Cameron leaned forward. 'I'd suggest that if any of us uncover the lead they picked up, they should pass it on to the others.'

Willoughby sneered and waved a dismissive hand at Cameron, who accepted his refusal with a frown before he looked at Reinhart.

'I agree with Willoughby,' Reinhart said. 'If I uncover this lead, I'll keep it to myself.'

Reinhart shook a fist for emphasis and then stood up. He nodded to Broderick and without further comment he headed off.

The other men watched him until he walked through the door. Then Cameron raised his glass to the remaining men.

'And then there were four,' he said.

'Three,' Broderick said, standing up. 'Reinhart had the right idea. I'm not sharing anything I learn.'

He wavered for a moment before – with an

almost apologetic shrug – he walked to the door.

'I don't suppose it's even worth saying that now there are three?' Cameron said, looking at Willoughby.

'Nope,' Willoughby said. 'I'm obliged for the information, and so when I've collected the bounty on Lachlan I'll buy you a few whiskeys.'

Willoughby then headed to the bar where he looked around the still empty saloon room before he sloped off to the door.

When he'd left, Jonathon and Cameron looked at each other silently until Jonathon smiled.

'And then there were two,' Jonathon said.

'It would seem so,' Cameron said with an approving nod. He glanced at the door. 'Then again I hardly expected that the five of us would ride off together in search of Lachlan.'

'Neither did I. Although I noticed that Reinhart nodded to Broderick before he left. I figure that they'll form some sort of partnership.'

Cameron nodded. 'Those two have worked together before, and as for Willoughby, the only thing you can trust about him is that he always works alone.'

'There's one other thing you can always trust about him.' Jonathon chuckled. 'He'll have no idea about how to find Lachlan.'

Cameron leaned back in his chair. 'I see that you've had dealings with Willoughby before.'

'Sure, and he's a sneaky varmint who somehow ends up collecting a bounty more times than he ought to.' Jonathon leaned forward. 'Which means that when he rides out of town, he'll follow Broderick and Reinhart in the hope that they'll lead him to Lachlan.'

'I agree.'

'Which just leaves one question: what should the two of us do next?'

'I reckon we should follow Willoughby.' Cameron narrowed his eyes making Jonathon think that he was about to ask the question he'd been expecting ever since he'd revealed the 'Wanted' poster. 'I assume you don't have a problem with going after your brother?'

Jonathon spread his hands. 'Lachlan McKinley is my stepbrother and I haven't seen that no-account waste of skin for nearly ten years. If I have to kill him to get my hands on four thousand dollars, I won't lose sleep over it.'

'Two thousand dollars,' Cameron said. 'If we're going to work together for the first time, the two of will share the bounty equally.'

'Of course,' Jonathon said.

CHAPTER 2

Miguel Castillo dragged Scorpio Blake through the door of Fairmount Town's law office and threw him to the floor.

Only one man was within. He was sitting behind a desk facing the door with his hat lowered, so that Miguel could see only his shaggy beard.

'I'm looking for Sheriff Troughton,' Miguel said.

'Troughton's not here,' the man said.

Miguel waited for the man to stand up and deal with Scorpio, but he stayed sitting.

'Then who are you?'

'US Marshal Jake T. Devine.' He raised his head. Cold eyes considered him. 'Who are you?'

'Miguel Castillo. I'm a bounty hunter and I've captured someone who ought to interest you.'

Devine glanced at the sprawling prisoner, who

had yet to move since he'd been deposited on the floor.

'He won't,' Devine grunted. 'The only thing worse than the scum bounty hunters bring in are the bounty hunters themselves.'

Miguel snorted a laugh. 'I'm not arguing with you there. You have to be tough to bring in men like Scorpio Blake.'

Devine got to his feet. He stalked around the desk to stand over the prisoner, who he appraised with his upper lip curled with contempt before he looked at Miguel with the same level of scorn.

'What's he done?'

'I reckon he was involved with Lachlan McKinley.'

'Where's Lachlan?'

'I didn't even get close to Lachlan, but eliminating Scorpio ought to weaken him.'

Devine shook his head. 'So you were too yellow to take on Lachlan and you settled for bringing in this one.'

'I don't care what you think,' Miguel said, now tiring of trading words with the marshal. He glanced around the office. 'I'm sure that when he returns Sheriff Troughton will be pleased that I've dealt with Scorpio.'

'Except he's not here.' Devine advanced a long pace on Miguel. 'So you'll have to deal with me, bounty man.'

Miguel shrugged. 'In that case, you can make sure I get paid.'

Devine grinned. 'Obliged for the opportunity to pay you what you deserve.'

Devine glanced at the prisoner and so Miguel followed his gaze only to find that Devine was thrusting up a hand. In a moment the hand closed around Miguel's chin and he was pushed backwards until he slammed up against the wall beside the door.

'Get off me,' Miguel muttered. 'We're on the same side. We both want Lachlan brought to justice.'

'I don't side with scum.'

Devine thudded a low punch into Miguel's stomach that made him fold over. He kept hold of Miguel's chin and raised his head back up only to punch him again.

Then he released him and with his guts feeling like they'd been crushed, Miguel dropped to his knees where he dragged in long gasps of air. When the pain had receded, he looked up at Devine.

'I guess I won't get paid today, then. I'll just wait for Troughton.'

Miguel raised a knee and while supporting his weight on his thigh, he pushed himself to his feet. He swayed until he got his balance and then moved towards the desk, but Devine darted in seeking to grab his shoulder.

This time Miguel had enough time to react. He shoved Devine's arm away and launched a wild punch at Devine's face, but with an alarmingly quick reaction Devine raised a hand and caught his fist.

With a twist of the arm Devine swirled Miguel round to hold him from behind. Then, with his arm thrust up his back, he walked him across the office.

When they reached the desk, he bent him over it to slap his cheek down against the top.

'You just made a big mistake. Nobody threatens me.'

'I'm not threatening nobody except men like Scorpio, and maybe one day soon Lachlan will get what he deserves, too.'

Devine leaned closer to mutter in Miguel's ear. Devine's breath was hot against his neck, but it still made a chill run down his spine.

'The law will deal with Lachlan, and not a man who only goes after outlaws for money. So you're about to get what you deserve, bounty man.'

'What's that supposed to—?'

Devine raised Miguel's head only to clunk it back down on the desk with a blow that rattled his teeth. Miguel's vision was still swirling when Devine raised him back up and then hurled him over the desk.

Miguel hit the desk, rolled, and then slammed

down on his side on the floor where he continued rolling until he fetched up against a wall. He groaned and moved to get back up, but he failed to control his limbs and he flopped back down again.

He sensed Devine moving round the desk to stand over him, but then shuffling sounded on the other side of the office. A moment later two rapid footfalls thudded as Devine turned and moved away.

'What do you think you're doing, scum?' Devine demanded.

'I wasn't doing nothing,' Scorpio said with a shaking voice.

Firm footfalls sounded as Devine advanced on Scorpio.

'You were trying to escape my justice. Nobody does that.'

Miguel tried to use the distraction to get up, but he couldn't summon the strength to move. Worse, darkness invaded the corners of his vision and he sensed that he was only moments away from blacking out.

'Leave me alone,' Scorpio said. 'Miguel's handed me over to Sheriff Troughton.'

'He hasn't. I'm looking after you.' A slap sounded followed by a thud and a cry of pain. 'Now, where's Lachlan McKinley?'

'I'm not telling you nothing,' Scorpio said, his

voice rising in panic.

Devine chuckled, the sound seeming to come from a great distance as Miguel struggled to remain conscious.

'Wrong,' Devine said.

CHAPTER 3

'You were right,' Cameron said after they'd been riding for an hour. 'Willoughby is following Broderick and Reinhart, and they're heading to Fairmount Town.'

Jonathon nodded. The previous night they hadn't seen the other three manhunters again, but this morning they had picked up Willoughby's trail easily and before long they had found the trails of two other riders.

It was now obvious that these men were heading east, and Fairmount Town was two days' riding away along this path.

'I wasn't completely right,' Jonathon said. 'I thought that after your warning they'd be more cautious than that and seek out a different way to track down Lachlan.'

'None of those men are inventive. They'll just follow the same predictable path until they ride into more trouble than they can handle.'

'Unlike us, who are just following them.'

Cameron laughed. 'I reckon we'll be able to do better than they will.'

Cameron turned in the saddle to smile at him and although he didn't ask the question Jonathon had been expecting since they'd left Bear Creek, he decided to answer it.

'I don't have any special information on Lachlan's whereabouts or on what he might be doing.'

'I never thought you would have, but you once knew Lachlan and so you know more about how he'll behave than you think you do.' Cameron shrugged. 'And if all else fails, when he sees you again, the element of surprise might give us an advantage.'

'He'll certainly be shocked to see me. The last time I saw him was before he went bad and before I started in this line of business.'

'Were the changes in both your lives con-nected?'

Jonathon hadn't considered this possibility before, but he still shook his head.

'We both had our reasons for following our dif-ferent paths.'

'Then I'm pleased I'm riding with the brother who went after bounty and not with the one who went after banks.'

19

Jonathon smiled and with Cameron not pressing him for details, he felt a need to explain himself. So he talked about his early life and about Lachlan.

When he had been young, times had been hard, but he hadn't known that life could be any different and, as he had been blessed with caring parents, he had been contented.

Sadly, when he was seven years old his father, Maynard Lynch, had died while he had been away from home looking for work, and afterwards everything had changed for the worse. His mother had moved to Redemption City where she'd sought out any work that would keep them fed.

Life had been desperately tough until she'd met Owen McKinley, a widower. This man was nothing like Jonathon's real father, being surly and quick to anger as well as being in poor health.

Jonathon had been too young to understand why his mother wanted to spend time with such a man. Later, he was able to accept that she'd had few choices, and most of them were terrible, so she had taken the least worst option for them both.

Owen's only child, Lachlan, followed after his father in temperament and so for the rest of his childhood he and Lachlan had barely tolerated each other.

Later, as young men, they had exchanged words only rarely and they did that only because they happened to live in the same town and they couldn't avoid coming across each other.

When Lachlan's father and then Jonathon's mother had died in quick succession, Lachlan had moved on and so had Jonathon. He had sought his own path in life, which soon took him into man-hunting.

He hadn't given Lachlan another thought until a chance encounter with an old friend led to him finding out that Lachlan was serving time in Beaver Ridge jail.

Jonathon had retained just enough interest in his stepbrother's life to ask for more details, learning that Lachlan had tried to kill a man outside a saloon after an argument over a poker game. He had got seven years.

This detail made Jonathon break off from his story to consider.

'Lachlan's sentence must have ended around six months ago,' he said. 'From what you said, this bank raid happened around six months ago.'

'Then Lachlan must have turned back to crime as soon as he left jail,' Cameron said.

'That sure is quick and from what I remember about Lachlan, he was quick to anger, but slow in everything else.'

Cameron chuckled. 'So I was right. You do know more about him than you thought you did.'

'Perhaps I do, but my point was that attacking a

21

man after a poker game is something Lachlan would do. Robbing a bank the moment he came out of jail isn't.'

Cameron shrugged. 'Then I guess that's another thing about this mission that's yet to make sense.'

CHAPTER 4

'That's where I heard about Lachlan McKinley,' Miguel Castillo said, gesturing at the trading post with his bound hands.

Marshal Devine glanced at the post and then turned in the saddle to look down at Miguel.

'And yet you brought in only Scorpio Blake,' he said.

'I keep on telling you that I couldn't find Lachlan.' Miguel gulped. 'And what did happen to Scorpio?'

Devine licked his lips. 'While you were dozing he had himself some trouble.'

Devine glared at Miguel until he lowered his head. Then he tugged on the rope with which he'd bound Miguel around the chest and, at a steady trot, he headed towards the post.

Several horses were in the corral at the side of the post. So Devine took a circuitous route that let

23

him approach the building from that side.

When he reached the corral fence he dismounted and tethered his horse. Then he dragged Miguel closer, making Miguel glare at him with defiance.

'You're not getting any more out of me than what I've told you already, because what I've told you is all I know.'

'You look like a man who knows nothing.' Devine snorted. 'Tell me your story again. Then I'll free you.'

Miguel hunched his shoulders confirming that he didn't believe him, but with a faltering voice he repeated the story he'd related three times already.

'A whole heap of illegal trade goes on at this post. The owner, Frederick Stiles, passes on any information he overhears, for the right price. He tells outlaws about men who are looking for them and tells bounty hunters where outlaws have gone, but he won't talk to lawmen.'

'Frederick's a wise man. What did he tell you?'

'He said Lachlan had holed up in Lerado. I went there, but it was a deserted ghost town. I staked out the town for three weeks until Scorpio showed up. He mooched around and then went back along the way he'd come. I followed him, but when he caught sight of me I captured him. He wouldn't tell me what he was doing.'

Devine sneered. 'You're a waste of skin. You got

seen and you couldn't make him talk.'

Devine reached down to his boot and withdrew a knife. Then, with a single slash, he cut through the rope between Miguel's wrists.

Miguel flexed his hands as he backed away for a pace.

'Obliged that you kept your promise,' he said.

Miguel moved to leave, but Devine slapped a hand on his shoulder, spun him round, and shoved him towards the post.

'Now you're free, you can talk to your friend.'

Miguel stuck out a foot and stopped himself, but Devine bundled him on until they reached the door where he shoved him inside. He waited for a moment and then followed him through.

A quick appraisal of the room confirmed that only two customers were within. They were standing on either side of a table looking down into an open sack.

One man was pointing while the other man was shaking his head suggesting that a lively debate had been in progress involving a trade for the contents of the sack. Both men silenced as Miguel shuffled up to the counter.

Devine glared at the seller and his prospective customer, his intense gaze making both men lower their heads.

As Miguel rapped on the counter, Devine walked up to the table and peered into the sack.

Several jugs were within.

'Do they interest you?' the seller said. 'If they do, I have many more fine—'

'Go,' Devine said.

The seller bristled. 'But we haven't agreed on how much they're worth yet.'

Devine snarled and swept the sack aside, making the jugs spill out and smash on the floor.

'You have now.'

The seller opened his mouth to protest, but his potential customer was already scurrying for the door. He sighed and peered at the mess of broken crockery, finding one jug that was still intact, but a glance at Devine made him decide to ignore it and hurry after his customer.

Devine watched them until both men left the post. Then he kicked the intact jug aside making it crash against the wall and headed to the counter.

The noise made Frederick emerge from a back room. He looked at the broken crockery strewn about the floor, but then shrugged when he appeared to accept that it wasn't his property.

'What do you want?' he asked, looking from Miguel to Devine and then back again.

'I was here recently,' Miguel said. 'You told me about a man who had gone to Lerado, Lachlan McKinley.'

Frederick frowned. 'Don't remember doing that.'

Frederick glanced at Devine with a surly look that said he had only been stricken down with amnesia due to the presence of a lawman, and so Miguel directed an apologetic glance at Devine.

'Your friend's not being cooperative,' Devine said. 'Talk to him, bounty man.'

'This is US Marshal Devine,' Miguel said with a measured tone and his eyes wide with a warning. 'He wants answers and he won't leave until he gets them.'

Frederick gulped, confirming he'd heard about the marshal before and then shuffled up to the counter.

'He'll have to. I don't talk to lawmen.'

Miguel lowered his head and so Devine took a long pace closer to Frederick.

'Then you won't talk to anyone ever again, post man,' he said.

Frederick shrugged with apparent unconcern and then lowered a hand, but he didn't get a chance to reach for the weapon that he no doubt kept close at hand as Devine lunged over the counter. He grabbed Frederick's collar and yanked him forward.

'I don't know nothing about this Lachlan,' Frederick said, his voice high-pitched with concern. 'I really don't.'

'A pity.'

Frederick didn't reply, but Devine held on to

him until he began to shake. Then he bodily hauled him over the counter.

Frederick went sprawling on his knees, so Devine raised him to his feet and pushed him back against the counter. Frederick struggled in his grasp, but Devine held him until he accepted that he wouldn't be able to free himself and desisted.

Then, with a thin smile, Devine released him.

'Obliged,' Frederick murmured with relief. 'Threatening me wasn't going to make me reveal anything because I don't know anything about Lachlan other than that he once went to Lerado.'

Devine nodded. 'I'm not threatening you, post man.'

Devine rolled his shoulders and then lashed out with a fist, catching Miguel with a swiping blow to the cheek that sent him spinning away. The moment Miguel hit the floor, Devine was on him and dragging him up on to his feet.

Then, while Miguel was still doubled over, he turned him to the counter and ran him at it. Miguel's face slammed into the rim of the counter and he dropped away screeching in pain and spitting blood.

'Why did you do that?' Frederick said, aghast.

Devine stood over Miguel. 'I told you. I'm not threatening you.'

'Hurting him won't make me talk.'

'It will.' Devine slammed two hands down on

Miguel's back and raised him up so quickly his feet left the floor. 'When I've finished with him, I'll start on you.'

Frederick closed his eyes for a moment. 'In that case, wait.'

Devine set Miguel down on his feet. Miguel stumbled a pace to the side and he had to hold out his arms to regain his balance.

Devine waited until he had righted himself. Then he kicked his legs out from under him, sending him clattering back down on his side.

He swung back his foot to kick Miguel in the stomach, but then he lowered it.

'Talk,' he said.

'Lachlan came here around six months ago,' Frederick said. 'He was looking for someone.'

'Who?'

Frederick glanced at the sprawling Miguel and then shrugged.

'Scorpio Blake.'

'Why did he want him?'

'I don't know.'

Devine thudded a low kick into Miguel's stomach that sent him sprawling over on to his back. While Frederick pleaded with him to stop and Miguel murmured in pain, he walked around Miguel and kicked him in the side, sending him rolling back in the other direction.

'Why did Lachlan McKinley want Scorpio Blake

and why was Scorpio in Lerado?' he demanded.

'I don't know!' Frederick screeched.

Devine narrowed his eyes, but Miguel spoke up.

'He doesn't know nothing about Scorpio and his activities,' he said with defiant finality.

Devine swept back his foot, but then nodded and lowered it.

'He doesn't,' he said. He walked around Miguel until he could look down at his blood-streaked face. 'But you do.'

Miguel groaned while Frederick shuffled from foot to foot confirming he was right.

'Scorpio had been seen loitering around Lerado,' Miguel said with an exasperated sigh.

'The rest?' Devine said.

'That's the whole story.' Miguel raised his head to spit blood to the side. 'Lachlan wanted Scorpio. Scorpio was in Lerado.'

'Not much of a story. Give me a better one.'

Devine set his feet wide apart and rolled his shoulders, but Miguel made no attempt to move away. When Devine noted that for the first time Miguel was looking at him with confidence, he settled his stance.

Then Devine hurled his hand to his holster while twisting on the hip. His Peacemaker came to hand and in a moment he had it aimed at Frederick, who was edging his hand across the counter.

When Frederick saw Devine's reaction, he made a frantic lunge for his concealed weapon, but he didn't get to lay a hand on it as Devine blasted a slug through his forehead.

Frederick's head cracked back before he toppled over backwards. He had yet to hit the floor when Devine swung back to face Miguel.

'I have no other story to tell,' Miguel said with a gulp. 'I'd never heard of this Scorpio Blake before Frederick told me about him.'

'In that case, we're going to Lerado.' Devine holstered his gun and reached down to grab Miguel's jacket. 'Do you want to live to see it again?'

'I do,' Miguel bleated as Devine raised him and bundled him on towards the door. 'But it doesn't change the fact that I can't tell you anything more about Scorpio.'

'Then that's bad news for you.' Devine swung Miguel round to face him. 'Because sometimes living can be worse than dying.'

CHAPTER 5

'Do we follow Willoughby into town?' Cameron asked.

'No,' Jonathon said. 'He'll be trying to avoid Broderick and Reinhart and it'll be hard for two more people to keep out of sight of all three men.'

Cameron agreed with this plan and so they settled down on a mound that commanded a good view of Fairmount Town.

For the last two days they had followed Willoughby's trail. They had never got close enough to see him, but they figured that he was several hours ahead of them.

As they had reached this spot in early afternoon, it was likely that Willoughby had arrived in town before noon. Broderick and Reinhart should have arrived even earlier, which gave them long enough to have made progress.

As the day wore on with no sign of any of the

three men leaving town, the urge to know what was happening made Jonathon and Cameron wander around impatiently and grumble to each other. That grumbling grew when later a train trundled into view.

With this development providing their quarries with a way to leave town without them noticing, they agreed to head into Fairmount Town.

They took a route that let them intercept the train after which they rode along on the other side to the town. When the train drew up at the station they moved into a position where they could see the passengers.

Only a few people boarded the train and none of them were their quarries. They still waited until the train left the station before they moved on to a stable on the edge of town.

While they were dealing with their mounts, Cameron pointed out two horses.

'Willoughby's horse isn't here, but those are Broderick's and Reinhart's,' he said.

'Then we should leave before they come back to the stable,' Jonathon said.

'We should, but not before we've at least learnt something useful.'

They slipped outside where they loitered by the building in the shadows, choosing a position that let them see most of the town.

Fairmount Town had two saloons and it was

likely that their quarries were seeking out information in one of them. As the saloons were on opposite sides of the main drag and they had large windows, they accepted that they would be seen if they approached either of them.

Jonathon pointed at the bank that stood beyond one of the saloons.

'The only thing I've learnt from this venture is that you were right,' he said. 'The bank is so small it was hardly worth raiding.'

'I know,' Cameron said. 'It looks after money only for the townsfolk and then not for all of them.'

'It's strange that it's not well supported.'

Cameron shrugged. 'It's not that odd. The townsfolk lost faith in their bank because of what happened to the previous one. If I remember right, it burnt down.'

Jonathon edged forward so that he could see down the length of the main drag, and he noticed a gap between two buildings beyond the saloon.

'That looks like the sort of place where a large bank might once have stood. Come on. Let's check it out.'

'There's no point. It has nothing to do with what's happening now, and if we wander around down there, Broderick and Reinhart might see us.' Cameron pointed at the stable. 'In fact, I reckon we've pushed our luck enough already and we should leave.'

'Back in the stable you said we shouldn't leave until we'd learnt something. The demise of the old bank might be that something.' Jonathon considered Cameron's sceptical expression. 'Then look at it this way: it'll be quicker to check out what's down there than to stand around here talking about it.'

Cameron gave a reluctant sigh and gestured for Jonathon to lead the way. Then they made their way to the back of the stable and along the backs of the buildings until they reached the gap.

With Cameron murmuring darkly about this risky and pointless endeavour, they stood at the corner of the area. It took Jonathon only a moment to confirm that although nothing remained other than a few marks on the ground, the space was large enough to have once contained a substantial building.

While Jonathon paced around kicking at the ground and shaking his head, Cameron watched the main drag.

'If another bank did once stand here, it burnt down a long time ago,' Cameron said. 'That makes it even more unlikely that it's connected to Lachlan's activities.'

Jonathon agreed, but he felt unwilling to give up on the only idea he'd had since they'd come to Fairmount Town. So when he noticed a man walking in their direction, he swung round to face him with the intention of asking him for information.

Then he saw that the man was heading straight for them. Jonathon beckoned to Cameron, who joined him in facing the newcomer.

'I've got a message from Broderick Trent and Reinhart Vane,' the man called after identifying himself as being Charles. 'They say that they're drinking in the saloon over there, so they'd be obliged if you'd use the other one.'

As Cameron and Jonathon cast irritated glances at each other, Charles grinned, clearly relishing their response.

'Tell them that it was inevitable we'd all start at the same place,' Cameron said. 'All that matters is who gets to Lachlan first.'

'They reckoned you'd say that. So they also wanted you to know that they've found out what the other bounty hunters learnt here. They all went to this trading post ten miles out of town that Lachlan McKinley had been known to use.'

'I'm obliged they've honoured my suggestion and shared information,' Cameron said through gritted teeth.

'There's more. They don't plan to go there. They're more interested in Scorpio Blake. He was found dead this morning with a bullet between his eyes.'

'Who's he?'

'Scorpio lived around these parts even before we had a town, but six months ago Lachlan was asking about him and he's not been seen since.'

Cameron nodded slowly. 'We appreciate the information. Tell them that if we learn anything useful, we'll be sure to pass it on.'

Charles laughed. 'They said that they don't reckon that's likely.'

Charles waited for a retort, but Cameron didn't reply and so with a disappointed shrug he started to turn away, but Jonathon raised a hand, halting him.

'Did a bank once stand here?' he asked.

'Yeah,' Charles said with a bemused shrug. 'It burnt down eight years ago during a bank raid and a whole heap of money got stolen. It was never found and so nobody here trusts banks no more.'

'Who raided it?'

'This bandit, Wayne Jackson, did it, but it didn't do him no good. He got trapped inside and died in the fire, while the rest of his men got rounded up within weeks.'

'And now, eight years on, Lachlan is a wanted man after he raided the new bank in Fairmount Town.'

'Sure.' Charles narrowed his eyes. 'Are you saying that's important?'

Jonathon smiled. 'Broderick and Reinhart have

told us what they're investigating. We're repaying them by letting them know what we're investigating.'

Charles nodded, although his narrowed eyes suggested that he didn't believe that Jonathon had told him anything useful. Then, with a shake of the head, he sloped off back to the saloon.

'Why did you tell him that?' Cameron asked when Charles had disappeared from view.

'Clearly they've decided to play games with us by telling us what they know,' Jonathon said. 'I decided to see what they'll do with the information we've gathered.'

'I agree that they're trying to rile us up so we'll act recklessly and get ourselves killed like the other bounty hunters did, but we have no information. There's no connection between the two bank raids.'

'Then that's even better as it won't help them.' Jonathon winked. 'And I didn't tell Charles about the important piece of information I've just picked up. Lachlan served time in jail for trying to kill a man. That man was Scorpio Blake and Scorpio's just been found shot up.'

Cameron smiled. 'Now that sure is interesting, and Broderick and Reinhart probably don't know about that yet.'

Jonathon nodded. 'So what are we going to do about it?'

Cameron moved forward until he was in a position where he could watch Charles slip into the saloon.

'I'm not getting drawn into playing games with those men. If the other manhunters went out to this trading post, then that's where we should go.'

Cameron took a long pace towards the saloon and rolled his shoulders, making Jonathon think that despite his comment, he would storm across the main drag and make Broderick and Reinhart regret their impudence. Then, with a shake of the head, he appeared to dismiss the matter and turned on his heels.

At a determined pace, Cameron walked off towards the stable. Jonathon watched him depart.

Despite Cameron's lack of enthusiasm, an old instinct that he had learnt to trust told him that the bank raid eight years ago was connected to the more recent one, although he couldn't see how right now.

He cast a last look around the gap between the buildings. Then, with a reluctant sigh, he followed Cameron.

CHAPTER 6

Sundown was an hour away when Jonathon and Cameron approached the trading post.

Their first sighting of it made both men draw to a halt. The building had been reduced to a smouldering ruin.

The wisps of smoke that still rose up suggested that the fire had consumed the post recently, as did the fact that Charles hadn't appeared to know about it when he'd relayed Broderick's message.

'So now we've come across another burnt-out building,' Jonathon said.

'Except there's no connection between this fire and the old bank burning down,' Cameron said with a weary air.

'Of course there isn't. That incident happened eight years ago and it isn't important. This building has just burnt down and it has to be relevant.'

This comment made Cameron smile before he hurried his horse on. Jonathon trotted on to join him, but when they drew up in front of the building he saw that they were as likely to find anything useful here as they had when they'd visited the site of the old bank.

All that remained was a heap of charred timbers. They both still dismounted and paced around the building.

'What do you reckon?' Cameron asked when they'd completed a tour of the site and returned to their horses.

'If this was an accident, an alarm would probably have been raised, but as there was no suggestion that anyone in Fairmount Town knew about it, I'd assume this was deliberate.'

'Agreed, and that means there could be bodies lying under all this burnt wood.'

Jonathon winced. 'If they are, I don't reckon that uncovering them will do us much good, in all ways. The only thing we can take from this is that someone is ahead of us and they're making sure that nobody follows them by destroying whatever evidence they've picked up.'

'Willoughby Jeffries?'

'I've never known Willoughby to be ahead of anyone. This is more likely to be Broderick and Reinhart's work. We didn't come here directly so they had enough time, and they could have told us they were following up Scorpio Blake's death to disguise their true intentions.'

Cameron nodded. Then, while sporting a thoughtful expression, he moved away and embarked on a slow walk around the vicinity.

He was clearly looking for tracks. As he was more skilled at finding them than Jonathon was, Jonathon left him to roam and moved closer to the burnt-out post.

He saw nothing of interest amongst the remnants, but when he located what he reckoned had once been the door he found a dark stain on the ground. He searched around and found smaller marks further away from the post, their spacing suggesting they were bloodstains made by someone hurrying away.

He gestured to Cameron only to find that he had already found something of interest and it was further along the path that the stains followed.

'There was a scuffle over here,' Cameron called. 'Then a rider moved off while dragging something along behind him.'

'From the look of these bloodstains, it could have been a body,' Jonathon said.

He moved on until he joined Cameron, confirming they had both found the same set of tracks. Then they mounted up and set about finding out where they led.

They had ridden along for around a half-hour

when the sun dropped behind low cloud, after which Cameron found it hard to follow the tracks and their progress slowed.

When the light level dropped even more, Jonathon was wondering if they should call a halt to their search for the day, but then Cameron drew to a halt and pointed ahead.

Jonathon followed his gaze to a bump a hundred yards ahead. Both men winced and then hurried on.

When they drew up, they stood on either side of the hunched-over form of a body. Jonathon dismounted and turned the body over, finding that the victim had been shot between the eyes, although he had clearly suffered before being killed.

His hands were bound together, his clothes were in tatters, and raw scuff-marks coated his visible skin. Trailing away from his wrists was a length of rope.

Behind the body, the furrow in the ground that they had been following suggested that the man had been dragged along behind a horse. The trail had been continuous since leaving the post and so he had been dragged for several miles until he had been cut free and dispatched.

'So could this be the fate that awaits us all?' Cameron said with a sorry shake of the head.

'There's no reason to think that.'

'There is.' Cameron tipped back his hat. 'This man is Miguel Castillo, the last bounty hunter to go after Lachlan.'

CHAPTER 7

Two men had just ridden into Lerado.

While lying on his belly Devine watched them from behind a heap of stones that stood on the edge of town and which had once been a wall of the town's bank. He had chosen this spot as being the most ideal for letting him see anyone approaching the ghost town.

It also let him watch most of the town, not that there was much to see as the fire that had ravaged the town two years ago had reduced nearly all of the buildings to mere skeletons. The most intact building was the mission, the only other stone-built building in town, and even then it lacked a roof.

As Devine had done earlier, the two men investigated the mission first and, like him, they emerged shortly afterwards shaking their heads. Then they stood in the centre of the town and with their hands on their hips they looked around.

They ran their gazes over the numerous unpromising places to explore until with a shrug to each other they set off towards the edge of town. They moved slowly while looking around and their meandering path took them towards the bank where Devine was hiding.

Devine lowered his head. Then he shuffled along to a higher stretch of wall where he could stand up while still remaining behind cover.

As the men moved closer they chatted to each other, identifying themselves as being Broderick and Reinhart.

'He has to have come here,' Reinhart said.

'Sure,' Broderick said. 'He headed this way and it was just one man, so it has to be Lachlan.'

'Or Willoughby.'

Broderick snorted a laugh. 'Willoughby is always behind everyone and either way, it's not like him to drag a man to his death, so who else could it be but Lachlan?'

Reinhart murmured in an uncommitted manner, the sound coming from only a few yards away. So with a long step Devine moved to the side to stand behind a lower length of wall where he could level his gun on the nearest man.

'US Marshal Jake T. Devine,' he said.

Broderick swirled round to face him and stepped back in surprise.

'What are you doing here?' he asked.

'The same as you.' Devine raised his gun a mite. 'Leave.'

Broderick shook his head. 'We're not leaving Lerado until we've worked out where Lachlan McKinley went after he came here.'

'Then you'll never leave.'

'We will.' Broderick gestured out of town. 'A man got killed back along the trail and we reckon his killer just has to be Lachlan and that he had to have come here.'

'The dead man is Miguel Castillo, a bounty man like you two.'

Broderick licked his lips. 'You're right that we're manhunters, and so while we stay here I reckon you should do what a lawman needs to do and track down Miguel's killer.'

Devine chuckled and then paced along until he reached a low stretch of wall. He strode over it to move closer to the two bounty hunters.

'You're hoping I'll ride off into a heap of trouble and make your mission easier.'

'Sure,' Broderick said with a grin.

'I like the way you think.'

Broderick shrugged. 'Miguel is just the latest in a long line of men who have headed to Lerado in search of Lachlan and ended up dead. We intend to make sure that this time it's Lachlan who bites the dust.'

Devine moved on and then circled round the men while looking them up and down.

'Then stay out of my way,' he said when he returned to standing before the ruined building. 'This is my side of town.'

'We'll remember that.' Broderick smirked and then with a glance at Reinhart he backed away. 'Keep on the lookout for Lachlan and keep yourself safe, Marshal.'

'Keep on the lookout for whoever killed Miguel, bounty man.' Devine chuckled. 'When you figure out who did it, come looking for me.'

CHAPTER 8

'I'm obliged to you for bringing back the body,' Sheriff Troughton said when he returned to the law office after examining Miguel's body.

'We figured we had to do that for one of our fellow bounty hunters,' Cameron said.

Cameron glanced at Jonathon, presumably warning him not to mention that they'd only decided to return to Fairmount Town as it had become too dark to follow the trail Miguel's killer had left.

'I've never seen any sign of men like you helping each other before, especially when such a large bounty is on offer.'

Cameron sat on the corner of Troughton's desk and smiled.

'Despite Miguel having joined the list of men who have failed to collect that bounty, we intend to succeed. The only question on our minds is the small matter of who'll pay us.'

Troughton glanced aside suggesting that Cameron had raised a matter that concerned him, too.

'I can't answer that,' Troughton said levelly. 'The bounty was posted anonymously shortly after the bank raid.'

'Can I take it from your low tone that you think there's something odd about that?'

Troughton nodded. 'Nothing about the situation makes sense. Although Lachlan got away with only a few hundred dollars, a week later the details arrived from a lawyer of a bounty being posted for his capture.'

'I assume that wasn't some kind of twisted joke and the money is actually available?'

'It's available. That's the only thing about this that can be trusted.'

'What don't you trust?'

Troughton moved round his desk and sat down. He rocked his head from side to side as if debating whether to answer.

'For a start, the raid was carried out by a masked man,' he said after a while. 'It's not unusual for a raider to hide his features, but this one told everyone he was Lachlan McKinley.'

'So you're saying that it's by no means certain that the man who robbed the bank was actually Lachlan, and even if it was him, he must have stolen something that's a lot more valuable than anybody knows about?'

Troughton rubbed his jaw and then nodded. 'That sums up my thoughts on the matter. Lachlan's crime doesn't justify that level of bounty, so there has to be more to this than just one small raid on one small bank.'

'That may be so, but the growing heap of dead men who have tried to collect that bounty would suggest Lachlan's a dangerous man.'

'It doesn't follow that Lachlan killed them all.'

Troughton then bit his bottom lip, suggesting he'd said more than he'd intended to. He gestured to the door, inviting them to leave.

'Who do you suspect?' Cameron asked while standing up.

'I don't.' Troughton frowned and then stood up and moved round his desk to face Cameron. 'While I was away, US Marshal Jake Devine was in town and he was showing an interest in Lachlan. It wouldn't surprise me if he's involved.'

Cameron raised a surprised eyebrow. 'In killing Miguel Castillo, the other bounty hunters and Scorpio Blake?'

'Scorpio was probably Lachlan's work when he completed the job he'd started eight years ago. I just mean that whenever Devine's around, the bodies always start piling up. Some say he's the finest lawman around and some say he's the worst. Most just try to avoid him.'

'In that case, we'll keep a lookout for him, and we're obliged for your help.'

Troughton shrugged. 'I only helped you because you brought in Miguel. I wasn't so helpful to the two bounty hunters who left town earlier today.'

Cameron nodded and moved to head to the door, but Jonathon stepped forward and spoke up for the first time.

'You did right to talk to us,' he said. 'We may be going after Lachlan for the bounty, but I'm Lachlan's stepbrother and I have a personal interest in working out what's going on here.'

'Understood.'

'So there's one final matter: is there any connection between Lachlan's recent raid and Wayne Jackson's raid on the old bank eight years ago?'

Cameron expelled an irritated blast of air making Troughton glance at him oddly before he turned back to Jonathon and shook his head.

'There's no similarity at all. Wayne led an organized gang of bandits.'

'Was Lachlan or Scorpio linked to that raid?'

'Lachlan wasn't, but whenever there was trouble in town Scorpio was usually involved, and that raid was one of the worst things ever to happen here.'

'So it was the sort of crime that could result in a large bounty being offered?'

Troughton looked aside as he appeared to think back.

'If I remember right around four thousand dollars was stolen, so I doubt it would have encouraged a bounty of the same size. Besides, all the raiders were tracked down without a bounty being posted thanks to me, a determined posse, and . . .' Troughton clicked his fingers and then looked at Cameron. 'Now I know where I've met you before. You were one of the men who joined in the search for the bandits.'

'I was in the area at the time,' Cameron said with a shrug, 'but there was no bounty on offer, so I moved on.'

Troughton sneered. 'And that's why you're lucky I've helped you as much as I have.'

With that, Troughton moved away and busied himself elsewhere in the office. Cameron glanced at Jonathon and sighed, seemingly acknowledging the question Jonathon would ask him when they left the office.

Jonathon decided not to keep him waiting. Once they were outside, he turned to him.

'You didn't mention that you've conducted business here before,' he said.

'That's because the earlier raid has nothing to do with our search for Lachlan,' Cameron said with a low tone.

'So you keep telling me, but the connections keep mounting up. Now we know that eight years ago four thousand dollars was stolen and it was never recovered, and the bounty on Lachlan is for the same amount and it was posted anonymously.'

Cameron pointed at him. 'Leave this, Jonathon. That's a coincidence, not a connection. You'll be telling me next that the bank raid twenty years ago in Lerado is connected to Lachlan.'

'I won't do that.' Jonathon smiled. 'I've never heard of this raid in Lerado.'

Cameron glared at him, seemingly preparing for a lengthy argument, but then he snorted a laugh.

'Let's get some rest,' he said. 'There's nothing else we can accomplish tonight.'

Jonathon agreed with that and so they sought out rooms for the night.

The next day they set off early and headed to the burnt-out trading post. They soon picked up the trail they had followed the previous day and they moved along it until they reached the spot where they'd found Miguel's body.

Cameron rooted around until he found the trail of the rider who had dragged Miguel from the post. In the better light he also found other recent trails, which made both men smile before they rode on.

The route the tracks took after leaving the post was straight and they headed broadly westward. So, when they had continued along the same path for another few miles, Jonathon turned to Cameron.

'Where do you reckon this trail might take us?' he asked.

Cameron didn't reply immediately and he shook his head several times as if he was already irritated by this conversation before it had begun.

'If our quarry continues in the same direction, after another half-day we'll ride through a ghost town.' He turned to Jonathon. 'It used to be a thriving town, but two years ago a fire destroyed it and the townsfolk moved to Fairmount Town. It's called Lerado.'

Jonathon shrugged and passed up the opportunity to mention Cameron's earlier taunt. The bank raid that had happened there couldn't be connected to a man who had been only a child twenty years ago.

Despite that, he couldn't stop his thoughts from dwelling on the two more recent raids. In the past he had often found his quarries after following up tenuous connections, and so he couldn't dismiss this matter until he had proved that the older raid wasn't connected to the more recent one.

More worryingly, he couldn't shake off his concern about Cameron's failure to admit he had been involved in the aftermath of the earlier raid.

He was still in a pensive mood when Cameron broke him out of his reverie to report that they were approaching Lerado.

A few miles further on, they caught their first

sight of the town. When they were close enough to confirm that it was a derelict ghost town, they stopped to debate tactics.

'We don't know for sure that Lachlan came here,' Jonathon said. 'All we do know is that Miguel's killer came this way.'

Cameron nodded. 'I agree that we don't know whether Lachlan killed Miguel, but we have to head there and check it out.'

Jonathon considered the flat terrain between them and the town.

'I wonder how many of the bounty hunters who have died looking for Lachlan stood here wondering why he had come to this place.'

'I'd guess it was some of them, so let's try to avoid making the same mistakes that they made.'

Jonathon smiled and so with that they moved on cautiously. They were still a few hundred yards away from the town when Jonathon saw movement amidst the derelict buildings.

Broderick Trent ran out from behind what looked like an old mission before disappearing amidst the wreckage of a collapsed building. A moment later gunfire blasted and Reinhart Vane scampered into view and took the same path that Broderick had.

Reinhart ran for several paces before another gunshot ripped out. He stumbled and dropped to his knees. Then he keeled over on to his chest.

'It looks like Reinhart and Broderick aren't faring any better than the rest did,' Jonathon said.

Cameron turned to Jonathon and gave a wry smile that acknowledged that if their rivals were facing trouble, it was tempting to leave them to their fate. Then, with a shake of the head, he hurried his horse on.

Jonathon speeded up to ride alongside him and they galloped on until they reached the edge of town. They drew up beside the only standing stone wall of an old building and scurried under cover.

With cautious movements they raised themselves to peer over the low wall and then trained their guns on the mission. Since Reinhart had dropped to the ground he hadn't moved again and neither had Broderick showed himself.

Silence dragged on for several minutes and so Cameron got Jonathon's attention and whispered a quick suggestion. When Jonathon nodded, Cameron put a hand to his mouth.

'Hey, Broderick,' he shouted. 'How's your investigation into Scorpio Blake's demise going?'

Jonathon chuckled as they awaited Broderick's response.

'Quit gloating, Cameron,' Broderick called. 'I could do with some help over here.'

'I thought you worked alone.'

'I hope you still find this situation amusing

57

when you're the next one to get shot up.'

Cameron glanced at Jonathon, who nodded and so he replied with a more conciliatory tone.

'In that case, what's going on here?'

'We figured out who killed Miguel Castillo and probably Scorpio, too.'

'Explain.'

Broderick raised himself briefly and then ducked down again.

'Cover me and I'll come over there and tell you everything.'

Jonathon reckoned Broderick must be desperate to let his opponent know his intentions, but he and Cameron did as Broderick had requested and blasted lead at the mission. A moment later Broderick leapt to his feet and ran towards them while firing in the same direction.

He covered half the distance to them at a brisk trot, but when he'd fired off six shots he thrust his head down and concentrated on sprinting for safety. He was ten paces away from the wall and Jonathon was waving him on when a gunshot tore out from the mission.

Broderick cried out and toppled over to lie face down in the dirt. Jonathon and Cameron both ducked down, but when no further gunfire sounded and Broderick didn't join them, they both edged up.

Broderick hadn't moved since he'd been shot

and the large patch of blood on his back confirmed he wouldn't do so again.

'Who's out there?' Jonathon murmured.

Cameron shrugged, but then, as if in reply to his question, a strident voice called out from the mission.

'This is US Marshal Jake T. Devine. Come out or die.'

CHAPTER 9

'We didn't come here to look for you,' Cameron shouted.

He waited, but when Devine didn't reply, he glanced at Jonathon.

'I haven't even seen Devine and he shot up Broderick and Reinhart with ease,' Jonathon said. 'So the marshal must be in a good position in the mission and it'll be risky to go for our horses.'

'I agree, but surrendering to this man could be even more risky.'

Based on what Sheriff Troughton had told them, Jonathon couldn't argue with that, but he took comfort from the fact that they were dealing with a lawman, after all. Even better, Broderick and Reinhart were the kind of men who could have given Devine good cause to kill them.

'Wish me luck,' he said to Cameron and then holstered his gun.

'Luck,' Cameron said, although he made no move to join him.

Jonathon stood up and moved out from their cover into full view of the mission with his hands spread out at chest level. Devine didn't respond and so he walked towards the building.

He was approaching Reinhart's body when he saw a gap in the mission wall above the open doorway. He judged that Devine could have fired through that gap and so he stopped and faced it.

Confirming his theory, Devine called out from behind the mission wall.

'Get your friend out here,' he demanded.

Jonathon didn't reckon he could get Cameron to comply, but the fact that he hadn't been fired upon had already made him move into view. With his hands raised Cameron walked slowly until he joined Jonathon.

The two men waited while shuffling sounded within the mission as Devine made his way back down to ground level. Then he paced through the doorway and faced them.

'We've done as you asked,' Jonathon said. 'Now why did you kill these two men?'

'You don't ask the questions,' Devine said. He walked sideways to stand beside Reinhart's body and kicked him over on to his back. He nodded and then spat on Reinhart's face. 'What are you doing here?'

Jonathon was about to say that they were bounty hunters who were on the same mission as the two dead men, but Devine's sneering expression when he looked up from the body made him shrug.

'I'm Jonathon Lynch and I'm looking for Lachlan McKinley,' he said. 'He's my stepbrother.'

Devine turned to Cameron. 'And you?'

'I'm Cameron Morgan, Jonathon's friend,' Cameron said, seemingly catching on to Jonathon's thought that they shouldn't mention they were bounty hunters.

'Your friend's brother is scum.'

'I know,' Jonathon said before Cameron could reply. 'That's why I need to find him and stop him before he commits more crimes.'

Devine pointed a warning finger at Jonathon and then at Cameron.

'You can find him, but I'll stop him.'

With that, Devine backed away and then turned to head back into the mission. As he walked inside he whistled tunelessly leaving Jonathon and Cameron to glance at each other and then follow him.

Broderick's and Reinhart's horses were standing at the far end of the mission. A fire had been set but not lit in the centre of the ravaged interior, suggesting that the men had made camp here before the gunfight.

Devine headed to the two horses and riffled

through Broderick's and Reinhart's saddlebags. He located a rolled-up package, which he tossed towards them, after which he hunkered down and set about lighting the fire.

'We reckoned Lachlan came this way,' Cameron said. 'The smoke from a fire could attract him.'

Devine's only answer was to glance up and smile. Then he stepped back from the fire as flames started to spread.

Cameron shrugged and picked up the package, which he unwrapped to reveal strips of beef.

'The bounty men didn't have much worth taking,' Devine said.

Cameron sat down and poked the food apart. 'This will be enough to feed us for a while, but I have no idea how long it'll be before Lachlan checks out this place, if he ever does.'

'Ask Lachlan's brother.'

Cameron looked at Jonathon who moved on to sit with him beside the growing fire.

'I don't know about Lachlan's recent move-ments,' Jonathon said, 'other than that people who head this way in search of him end up dead.'

Devine threw another branch on the fire. 'Then stay out of my way and you'll be fine.'

Cameron nodded, but Jonathon narrowed his eyes.

'Are you saying that if we let you deal with Lachlan, we'll be fine, or that you're responsible for all the people who have died out here?'

Devine licked his lips. 'Both.'

'That's impossible!' Jonathon snapped, leaping to his feet. 'Bounty hunters have been going missing for months.'

'Don't care about them, but I've only been here for a week.' Devine chuckled. 'If I'd been here longer, I'd have got to the others before Lachlan did.'

Jonathon and Cameron exchanged surprised looks before they both turned back to Devine.

'Are you saying you killed Miguel, too?'

'He got in my way. Nobody does that.' Devine gestured at the package. 'Now hand over some food and we can enjoy a nice, pleasant meal together.'

Cameron shot a warning glance at Jonathon, who rocked from foot to foot before with a sigh he sat down and did as Devine had requested.

For the next fifteen minutes Jonathon and Cameron sat quietly and chewed on their beef while Devine speared his meat with a knife and wolfed it down. Then Devine lay on his back with his head resting on Reinhart's saddle and his hat drawn down over his eyes.

Cameron sat on the other side of the fire, while Jonathon climbed up a heap of rubble beside the door to look out through the gap in the wall that Devine had used to fire upon Broderick and Reinhart.

For the next hour he kept watch without incident until Cameron relieved him. Before the sun set they swapped duties one more time, with Devine not offering to help.

With the fire banishing the darkness within the mission but not helping them to see further afield, in low voices Jonathon and Cameron exchanged views on what kind of precautions they should take.

'You were right that we don't know if Lachlan will ever come to Lerado,' Jonathon said. 'Even if he does, we don't know how long we'll have to wait.'

Cameron nodded. 'In that case, we should be cautious, but we should still make sure we get plenty of rest. I'll take one end of town and you take the other.'

Jonathon nodded and so they moved to leave, but that made Devine raise his hat for the first time in hours.

'What have Lachlan's brother and Jonathon's friend decided?' he asked.

'We're leaving to keep watch for Lachlan,' Jonathon said. 'If you don't want to join us, you can guard the mission.'

'You're going nowhere.'

Jonathon set his hands on his hips. 'We're not your deputies, so you can't stop us from deciding how we want to proceed.'

'Then try to leave.' Devine edged his hand towards his holster. 'Another two bodies littering up the town won't frighten off Lachlan.'

Jonathon glanced at the door and then at Cameron, who shook his head.

'We can't just sit in here waiting for someone who may never come,' Jonathon said.

'He'll come.' Devine patted his holster. 'If the food runs out before he arrives, you two can draw lots to decide which one we'll eat.'

Jonathon and Cameron both snorted laughs, but Devine merely considered them with cold eyes.

'You sound sure about Lachlan's plans,' Cameron said. 'Tell us what you've figured out.'

'Tell me what you know.'

Cameron shrugged. 'All we know is that Lachlan raided Fairmount Town's bank six months ago. We heard that he often used the trading post, so we went there. We found it burnt down and Miguel's body nearby, so we followed your trail to Lerado.'

Devine spat into the fire. 'Jonathon has scum for a brother and an idiot for a friend.'

Cameron lowered his head, but Jonathon's heart thudded in anger and he jerked forward meaning to advance on Devine and confront him. Then, with a shake of the head, a sense of self-preservation defeated his irritation and he dismissed the matter.

Jonathon settled his stance and so it was

Cameron who stepped forward, although he did so calmly.

'Right now that's all we know for sure,' Cameron said, speaking quickly. 'We're piecing together the rest.'

Devine raised an eyebrow requesting details, but Cameron's only reply was a sigh, presumably as he couldn't bring himself to mention Jonathon's theory.

'There's more going on here than just Lachlan's bank raid,' Jonathon said. 'The raid on Fairmount Town's bank eight years ago is connected and the fact that everyone is interested in Lerado suggests that whatever happened here twenty years ago could be connected, too.'

'So Lachlan's brother is an idiot, too,' Devine said. 'Even the dead scum out there figured out that much.'

Jonathon smiled, now feeling in control of the anger that had nearly made him confront Devine a few moments ago. He paced around the fire until he stood before Devine.

'We're leaving,' Jonathon said. 'Don't try to stop us.'

Devine narrowed his eyes as Jonathon sensed Cameron settling his stance behind him.

'I've got only one thing to say about that,' Devine said without concern. He winked. 'We've got company.'

Jonathon opened his mouth to snap back a retort, but then he registered what Devine had said. A moment later footfalls sounded outside.

He turned and hurried back around the fire. Cameron turned to the door while Devine didn't move from his position lying on the floor, although he was already facing the door.

The footfalls approached and then stopped. Jonathon and Cameron drew their guns and levelled them on the doorway, while from the corner of his eye Jonathon noted that Devine only kept his hand beside his holster.

Then the man outside coughed before he spoke up.

'This is Sheriff Troughton from Fairmount Town,' he called. 'Who's in there?'

'It's Cameron Morgan and Jonathon Lynch,' Cameron said with relief. 'We spoke with you in town yesterday.'

Troughton stepped in through the doorway and nodded to both men. Then he saw Devine and he came to a halt.

'I'm glad I've finally met you, Devine,' he said. 'I have some questions to ask you.'

'And if I don't answer them?' Devine said.

Devine stood up and took a long pace forward to face the sheriff through the flames, while Troughton moved into the mission to stand in front of the fire.

'You'll have to go back to Fairmount Town with me.'

'Then we have a problem.' Devine spat to the side. 'I'm not leaving the mission, lawman.'

CHAPTER 10

Devine rolled his shoulders, but Sheriff Troughton considered him benignly.

'I'm pleased that you've decided to stay, Devine,' Troughton said. 'It must mean that you're prepared to answer my questions.'

'I ask questions,' Devine said. 'I don't answer them.'

'Then you're right. We do have a problem.'

For long moments Devine looked into the flames and then smiled.

'I shot up Scorpio Blake when he tried to escape and I killed Frederick Stiles when he turned a gun on me. Miguel Castillo had too many secrets and Broderick Trent and Reinhart Vane came looking for revenge for Miguel.'

Troughton tipped back his hat. 'I'm obliged you provided some answers.'

'You didn't ask any questions.'

Troughton nodded. 'I guess I didn't. If that's the way you want to do this, someone torched Frederick's trading post.'

'Too many scum gathered there. They won't be doing that no more.'

'So what you're saying is that you had good cause to shoot up everyone who's died in my territory recently.'

Troughton hadn't intoned his comment as a question and so Devine gestured at the fire.

'I always have good cause. Now share our fire while we wait for Lachlan McKinley.'

'Lachlan will be long gone, if he ever holed up here.'

'These two are filled with wrong ideas, but they're idiots.' Devine snorted. 'What's your excuse?'

Troughton flared his eyes while he appeared to seek the right words for a retort, but as Jonathon could see that an argument was likely to erupt, he spoke up instead.

'Devine knows something about Lachlan's movements that he's not prepared to divulge,' he said.

Troughton shook his head. 'He may do, but why should I be interested in the opinion of a murderous lawman who's a worse threat to the peace in my county than the outlaws he shoots up?'

'Being as you asked so nicely,' Devine said

71

without concern. 'I know because twenty years ago I was in Lerado.'

'Twenty years ago Lachlan was a child,' Jonathon spluttered, unable to hide his disbelief. 'He wasn't involved in whatever happened here.'

Devine turned his cold gaze on Jonathon. 'Children see things.'

Jonathon nodded and then looked aside as he thought back.

His father had died around twenty years ago and it had been a few months before his mother met Owen McKinley in Redemption City. Back then he had been too young to be interested in where Lachlan's father had come from, but he could have lived in Lerado and Lachlan could have witnessed something that had drawn him back here.

How that fitted into the recent bank raid and his theory that the previous Fairmount Town bank raid was also connected, he couldn't see. So he listened intently when Troughton turned to him and started talking about the events in Lerado.

'I can't remember anyone ever mentioning Devine's involvement,' he said, 'but everyone from around these parts knows what happened here twenty years ago.'

When Cameron nodded, Jonathon had to sigh.

'So it would seem, but I'd like to know, too,' he said.

Troughton nodded. 'A group of men found an

abandoned wagon that had fallen into a crevasse in Saddle Pass. It had been there for a long time and on board was a locked casket, which they brought back to the town bank. It was opened and found to be filled with Mexican gold. Nobody knew how it had got there or who owned it, but the men soon realized that they were unlikely to be deemed the owners.'

'So they raided the bank and stole the gold?'

Troughton sighed. 'Sure. They weren't typical bank raiders. They were just decent men who'd had a lucky break that they thought would change their lives. When that chance was snatched away, they snapped.'

'I'd guess from your low tone that this story ended badly, both for the men and for the fate of the gold?'

'It did. The men holed up in Hangman's Gulch. They were given the option of surrendering, but they fought to the last.' Troughton shook his head. 'Worse, when the gulch was explored, the gold wasn't there and it's never been found.'

'So they probably buried it somewhere and, with the raiders all dead, nobody knew the location.'

Troughton shrugged. 'Either that, or someone escaped with it.'

'That's a sorry tale indeed, but how does Devine fit into this?'

Troughton spread his hands and then looked at

Devine, who took long moments to respond.

'Some men did escape from that pathetic attempt at an ambush in the gulch,' Devine said. 'With the gold still missing, I was tasked with rounding them up. The worthless scum didn't last long.'

'So you killed them all before anyone could confess,' Jonathon said. 'As a result you didn't find the gold, and that means you failed.'

Troughton drew in his breath sharply, as did Cameron, and they had good cause as Devine tensed.

'I never fail,' he intoned.

'Twenty years on we're standing here discussing the fate of the gold that you were sent here to find. That sounds like a failure to me.'

Devine drew in his breath through his nostrils. Then, with long strides, he stormed around the fire and advanced on Jonathon, who stood his ground.

With alarming speed Devine reached him and hurled a round-armed punch at Jonathon's face. Jonathon raised an arm to block the blow, but Devine's punch was so powerful it brushed his arm aside and clattered into his cheek sending him down on one knee.

Jonathon shook his head and looked up only to find Devine's foot arcing round towards his face. He jerked his head away, but the boot still crunched into his chin knocking him on his back.

With his vision swirling he tried to get up before Devine could attack him again, but his limbs had gone numb and he failed to move. His ears were ringing, but he could still hear Troughton remonstrating with Devine.

'That's enough,' the sheriff declared.

'Lachlan's brother has got too many wrong ideas,' Devine muttered.

'You may not agree with him, but that doesn't give you the right to beat him.'

A heavy footfall sounded and Jonathon's vision came into focus to let him see the marshal looming over him, but then Devine straightened up.

'That had better not be a gun you've drawn on me, lawman,' Devine said.

'I'm just keeping the peace.'

Devine turned and considered Troughton along with the gun he'd drawn, although he was keeping it lowered and pointing to the side.

'You've got some guts, lawman. Nobody holds a gun on me and lives. So don't go thinking that your badge will protect you if you raise that gun.'

Troughton settled his stance. 'Except I don't reckon you'd harm another lawman.'

Devine looked Troughton over. When Troughton returned his gaze levelly, Devine snorted and then turned back to face Jonathon.

With a firm lunge, he grabbed Jonathon's jacket front and bodily dragged him up. Then he set him down on his feet.

'Obliged,' Jonathon said.

'Don't be. Only this lawman's badge is stopping you from suffering the same fate as your worthless brother will.'

Jonathon shrugged. 'I can accept that.'

Devine nodded and started to turn away, but then he swung back and thudded a pile-driver of a punch into Jonathon's stomach that made him drop down on his knees.

Jonathon folded over, struggling to drag air into his lungs. He was powerless to stop Devine hitting him again, but thankfully the marshal backed away and then pointed at each man in the mission in turn.

'I never fail,' he said.

Nobody replied and so Devine stalked back to his position by the fire. Troughton and Cameron came over to Jonathon and helped him back to his feet.

'What now?' Cameron asked Troughton.

'I have no idea whether Devine is right and Lachlan will come to Lerado,' Troughton said. 'But it'll do no harm to stay here tonight and review the situation in the morning.'

Jonathon and Cameron nodded, but Devine shook his head.

'Nobody leaves the mission,' he declared.

Troughton sighed and lowered his head, and as Jonathon shared the sheriff's lack of enthusiasm for prolonging the argument, he settled down beside the fire. Cameron joined him where he considered Devine warily.

For the next hour everyone sat quietly and presently Jonathon relaxed enough to doze for a brief period. Later, the other men started snoring.

As enough men were here to ensure that someone would hear anyone approaching the mission, he joined them in getting some restful sleep.

The next time he stirred light was shining down through the top of the roofless mission and someone was moving nearby. He came awake quickly and looked towards the noise, finding that Troughton was walking to the door to look outside.

'Trouble?' Jonathon asked.

Troughton turned to him and shrugged. 'It depends on how you look at it. Devine's gone.'

Jonathon flinched and looked in the other direction. The sheriff was right. Devine was no longer lying beside the fire.

Jonathon tried to feel relieved about this development, but he couldn't shake off the troubling thought that Devine had managed to leave the mission without any of them hearing him.

CHAPTER 11

'What's your plan now?' Jonathon asked Sheriff Troughton when they had confirmed that Devine had not only left the mission, but he had left Lerado, too.

'I'm not convinced that Lachlan will come here,' Troughton said. 'It doesn't seem that Devine really believed that either.'

Troughton nodded. 'It doesn't, but I reckon that's the way Devine works. He was just trying to get under our skins with his unreasonable demand, but that leaves us with the question of where Lachlan's gone. I'm open to suggestions, if you're minded.'

Cameron shrugged and turned away, but Jonathon didn't see anything wrong in sharing ideas with the lawman. So he looked out of town towards the north where the land grew higher and more rugged and which would probably provide plenty of places where Lachlan could have holed up.

'We could search for months without luck, so I guess the question that needs to be answered first is what do you reckon is going on here?'

'There's plenty about this situation that doesn't make sense, but I usually find that the simplest version of events is the right one. Lachlan got hold of some information about the location of the gold that went missing twenty years ago. He needed money to finance the search and he stole from the bank. Someone else knows what Lachlan is doing and they posted a bounty on his head to stop him.'

'It's possible, and all the dead bounty hunters who have gone after him would suggest they followed clues to Lachlan's location, which I'd guess is Hangman's Gulch.'

Troughton shook his head. 'You're not the first man to come up with the theory that during the shootout in the gulch the raiders buried the gold. So plenty of men have gone there, and yet the only ones to die are the manhunters who have gone after Lachlan.'

Jonathon smiled. 'Which would suggest the manhunters went to a different place.'

'Sure, and as there are no clues here as to where that place is, I reckon they went to Saddle Pass, the place where this whole sorry saga started.'

'You could be right. With no information available, I'd certainly look there.'

Troughton frowned and Jonathon reckoned the obvious question was on his lips as to whether they should leave together, but he didn't ask it and without further comment he turned away. As he headed to his horse, Cameron turned back to Jonathon.

'So the sheriff is going to scout around in Saddle Pass and hope he gets lucky,' he said. 'I reckon we can do better than that. We'll rest up here and wait for Lachlan to come to us, like Devine thought he would.'

Jonathon shook his head. 'I reckon Troughton was right. Devine was forcing us to stay just to provoke us, and either way, as he left last night, he proved that he didn't really believe Lachlan would come here.'

Cameron glanced around at the surrounding terrain, picking out a nearby elevated stretch of land to the east.

'Perhaps he only wants us to think that while he stakes out the town from up there.'

Jonathon glanced at the higher land and shrugged.

'He might be doing that, but Troughton has the better idea that Lachlan is looking for the gold, and he wouldn't be doing that here.'

Cameron sighed and then contemplated him

with his hands on his hips.

'I guess that when we agreed to ride together this moment was always going to come. I say we should stay and you say we should leave. So make your decision, but whatever you decide, I'm burying Broderick and Reinhart, and then I'm staying.'

Jonathon shrugged. 'I'll help you to bury them, but you'll have to give me a good reason to stay beyond Devine's statement that he thought Lachlan would return.'

'All I have is my belief that Lachlan will come here in search of the gold. Call it my instinct as a manhunter, like your instinct that the recent raid was connected to the older bank raid. If that's not good enough for you, you can go.'

Jonathon stepped back from Cameron. The previous night Cameron had made no attempt to defy Devine and he hadn't tried to help him when Devine had attacked him.

Clearly since they'd arrived here something had changed for him. Jonathon didn't know whether that was due to the presence of the lawmen, the recent deaths, or perhaps the fact that he had always viewed their partnership as a temporary one of convenience.

Jonathon glanced at Troughton who was now mounted up and setting off to leave town. He didn't want to ride with the lawman, but he also didn't want to ride alone or stay here.

'I'll back any hunch, but I don't see what you're basing your hunch on,' he said. 'So, I can't help but recall that last night you were the only one not to confront Devine, and that makes me think you're scared of him.'

Jonathon had hoped his taunt would anger Cameron and lead to a frank exchange of views about their next actions, but Cameron glanced away.

'Any sane man would be scared of Devine after what he did to Broderick and Reinhart, and the best way to avoid Devine is to deal with Lachlan quickly and collect the bounty.' Cameron smiled. 'I reckon I'll take the risk for four thousand dollars.'

'As you reminded me in Bear Creek, we agreed to share the bounty equally, so that's two thousand dollars.'

'Of course, but only if you stay.'

Jonathon frowned now that Cameron had delivered his ultimatum. He guessed that to risk ending their partnership over a hunch, Cameron must have a better reason to stay than the one he'd divulged, and that alone helped him to make his decision.

'I'm leaving,' he said, and with that he headed off to collect his horse.

By the time he was riding out of town after

Troughton, Cameron had dragged the bodies of Broderick and Reinhart together, but he broke off to nod to him.

Jonathon didn't acknowledge him and instead he hurried his horse on.

CHAPTER 12

The man was lying on his belly on the edge of the rise that looked down on Lerado. He was ten paces away from Devine and facing away from him as he looked to the north.

Strangely, the man was ignoring Troughton and Jonathon as they left town, and that intrigued Devine.

He stood up quietly and made his way closer to the man until he could see the area that he was watching. There was nothing of obvious interest in that direction and neither had Devine seen anything untoward since leaving Lerado earlier.

Devine aimed his gun at the man's back and then stomped his feet.

'See anything interesting?' he asked.

The man tensed and then raised himself as he prepared to turn around quickly while reaching for his gun.

'Who's asking?'

'US Marshal Jake T. Devine.'

The man groaned. Then he rolled over while sitting up, but he kept his hand away from his holster.

'I wasn't doing nothing. I'm Willoughby Jeffries and I was just wondering if it was safe to head down into Lerado.'

Devine stalked towards Willoughby to stand over him. Troughton and Jonathon were no longer visible while down in Lerado he could just make out movement as Cameron walked around town.

'So you've been watching out for trouble, have you?'

'I have, but I haven't seen nothing.' Willoughby shrugged. 'I didn't even see you until you sneaked up on me.'

Devine tapped a boot against Willoughby's leg.

'I didn't ask about what you haven't seen. Tell me what you have seen.'

'Nothing other than those two men leaving town.' Willoughby gave a hopeful smile. 'And there's another man lurking around in Lerado.'

'What's happening over there?' Devine gestured to the north.

'I don't know. I haven't—'

Willoughby didn't get to complete his denial as Devine lunged down, grabbed his jacket front, and dragged him closer.

'Talk.'

'When I arrived five men were watching the town,' Willoughby said with a tremor in his voice. 'They went north before first light and they haven't come back.'

'And the rest?'

'There's nothing more. I just don't want no trouble and so I was keeping a careful watch on everyone.'

Devine snarled and stood up straight, dragging Willoughby to his feet. Then he disarmed him and bundled him along to the edge of the rise.

The slope here was steep, but it was negotiable with care and so he walked Willoughby to a section where the first part of the slope was a sheer drop of twenty feet. Devine stood before the edge and gathered a firm grip around Willoughby's collar.

'Who were the five men who left first?' he demanded.

'I don't know,' Willoughby bleated.

Devine shoved Willoughby until he was leaning backwards over the edge with his feet scrambling for purchase on the loose ground.

'Who?'

'I can't tell you nothing. It was dark when I got here and I only heard them when they moved out. Then I saw them from a distance and later Sheriff Troughton and Jonathon Lynch left. That's all I know.'

Devine narrowed his eyes, but he didn't reply letting Willoughby register the mistake he'd just made. When Willoughby gulped, Devine shoved him backwards for another foot until all that was stopping him from falling was the grip he had of his collar.

'How do you know Jonathon Lynch?'

'He's a bounty hunter, like me.'

Devine sneered. 'There are two dead bounty men down in Lerado. I killed them.'

Willoughby winced and looked away from Devine's piercing gaze.

'That doesn't change nothing. I don't know who the men who went north are.'

'You were interested enough to keep looking that way.'

'I watch everything that goes on, but I don't know who they are or what they wanted.'

'A pity.'

Devine dragged Willoughby a mite closer and treated him to a wide smile. When Willoughby smiled in apparent hope of getting a reprieve, he opened his hand.

Willoughby wheeled his arms before he went tumbling away. A moment later a thud and a cry of pain sounded.

Devine leaned forward to watch Willoughby skitter down the slope. With frantic movements Willoughby thrust out his arms and after scrambling around he managed to grab hold of a root and still his progress.

Devine walked along the edge to a less steep stretch of slope and made his way down. When he was level with Willoughby, he walked towards him.

Willoughby murmured with concern. He stood up and backed away with his hands raised until he stumbled and went falling down on to his back.

'Leave me alone,' he wailed when Devine reached him. 'I don't know nothing about those men.'

'I thought you'd be all broken up. Talk or I'll take you back up there and throw you off the edge again.'

Willoughby looked around frantically for a way to escape, but the rest of the slope downwards was treacherous.

'I can't help you. All I do is follow people until I find things out about them and I've yet to find out anything about the men who were watching the town.'

Devine snarled and lunged down making Willoughby cringe away, but then he stilled his hand and opened it to present the palm to him. Willoughby looked at the hand with bemusement clearly wondering if Devine really was offering to help him to his feet.

'Take it,' Devine said with a thin smile splitting his bushy beard.

'You're accepting my word?' Willoughby said, aghast.

'No. I'm letting you use your talent. You'll follow them.' Devine licked his lips. 'If I like what you find, you won't get all broken up.'

CHAPTER 13

'We should reach Saddle Pass early tomorrow,' Sheriff Troughton said when he and Jonathon had made camp for the night. 'So I need to know what you'll do if we encounter any trouble there.'

Jonathon nodded. They had talked only briefly after he had joined Troughton to search for Lachlan and he hadn't expected the sheriff to trust him, especially when he was only joining him because he had no other clues to follow.

'I came in search of Lachlan for the bounty and I owe nothing to my stepbrother.' Jonathon frowned. 'On the other hand, Lachlan's the only family I have and I feel that I ought to do more than just bring him to justice.'

'Which begs the question of what will you do if Lachlan has found the gold?'

'It'll change nothing. I don't steal.'

Troughton rubbed his jaw and then nodded.

'I'll trust your word on that, but if you give me cause to doubt you, I'll treat you the same as I intend to treat Lachlan.'

'I can't argue with that. All I can offer is that you can trust me more than you can trust Cameron and the other men who have gone after Lachlan.'

Troughton smiled. 'And probably Devine, too.'

Jonathon nodded and with that agreement they settled down for the night. They spoke little for the rest of the evening and the next day they spoke only when Troughton pointed out the route they would take.

As promised, in mid-morning they approached the entrance to Saddle Pass.

'What's your plan?' Jonathon asked when Troughton rode towards the entrance with no sign that he would take any precautions.

'The pass is long and winding with numerous places where Lachlan could have gone to ground,' Troughton said. 'If we searched out every hiding-place it'd take us months. So we'll go to the place where the wagon was found and see if anyone has been there recently.'

'And if anyone has been there, it'll be suspicious as most people who search speculatively go to Hangman's Gulch?'

Troughton nodded and so they moved on to the entrance. Then Troughton directed them to stay on the north side of the pass where the slope was steep and often vertical.

Jonathon agreed that it was unlikely anyone would be holed up there, and they had a good view of the gentler slope on the other side.

For the rest of the morning they rode steadily, until around noon they reached an area where the pass widened. When they reached the widest point, Troughton called a halt.

He pointed to a ledge that was around a hundred feet above them. It looked no different to the numerous other rocky formations they had passed over the last few hours.

'A crevasse is on the other side of the ledge,' Troughton said. 'That's where the wagon was found.'

Jonathon backed his horse away so that he could have a better view of the area.

'Then it's a wonder the wagon was ever found. I can see no reason why anyone would go up there.'

'Apparently, the men were looking for a quicker route out of the pass and someone climbed up on to the ledge to look around.'

Jonathon sighed. 'Then I guess I ought to do the same so I can start making sense of this situation.'

Troughton nodded. 'I've already seen the crevasse. I'll scout around while you see the scene for yourself.'

Jonathon dismounted and searched for the best route up to the ledge. Numerous tracks and scuff marks led upwards and so he followed the most well-worn path that let him reach the ledge within a matter of minutes.

He paused for breath and then shuffled across the ledge to a gap in the rock that let him look down into the promised crevasse. From here he could see how the wagon had suffered its fate.

The top of the pass was another hundred feet higher than the ledge. The land up there appeared to be flat, so he figured that when the hapless wagon had come trundling along, the treacherous gash in the rock had probably only become visible at the last moment and it had swallowed it up.

He leaned as far over the ledge as he dared and peered down, but nothing of interest remained. So he moved back to the other side where he watched Troughton search for recent tracks.

Troughton was pacing around in a systematic manner, but he was shaking his head suggesting he hadn't had any success yet. So Jonathon did what the man who had originally come up here must have done and used the high vantage point to look further afield.

Then he saw something move.

The movement had been on the other side of the pass and the unexpected sight made him flinch. He wasn't sure what had moved and where exactly it had happened, and when several moments passed without him noticing anything untoward again he sat down.

He dangled his feet over the side of the ledge to give the impression he was acting in a casual manner. Then he looked to the left and right while from the corner of his eye he watched the other side of the pass.

He noted two unusual rock formations, with a massive boulder that looked like a man's face and another one that looked like a bird. Both were natural occurrences, but for a reason he couldn't fathom they gave him an odd feeling and they held his attention until he again saw something move.

This time he pinpointed the exact position of the movement and it came from between the two rocks. A man was lurking behind a boulder and he was bobbing up from time to time to watch Troughton.

Jonathon stood up and while maintaining his casual demeanour he moved to the other side of the ledge and peered into the crevasse before he made his way down the slope. When he reached ground level, he looked for tracks in an area where Troughton hadn't searched yet.

Ten minutes of steady pacing later, their paths crossed. Jonathon nodded to Troughton, and the sheriff stopped.

'No luck so far,' Troughton said.

'Don't react, but we have company,' Jonathon

said with a sorry shake of the head to give the impression to the watcher that their search was going badly. 'Someone is lurking around on the other side of the pass.'

Troughton tipped his hat back and then pointed up and down the pass as he adopted Jonathon's policy of looking as if they were exchanging innocent information.

'Where exactly?'

'There are two large rocks that look like a man's face and a bird. He's hiding behind a boulder between them.'

Troughton frowned. 'I haven't noticed those rocks, but I reckon I know the area you mean. We'll stay together and look as if we're searching for tracks, but we'll make our way towards our watcher.'

Jonathon rocked his head from side to side as if considering and then directed Troughton to take the lead. They walked towards the nearest rock formation, which let Jonathon note that when seen from ground level both of the rocks no longer presented such distinctive profiles.

He was still able to work out where their watcher had gone to ground. So with subtle directions to Troughton he ensured that they gave the impression they were merely working their way across the pass, while moving closer to the man's hiding-place.

Despite his precautions, Jonathon reckoned that their progress might still worry the watcher and sure enough, when they were three-quarters of the way across the pass, a gunshot blasted out. Dirt kicked ten feet ahead of them suggesting it had been a warning shot.

'No nearer,' the man called. 'Just head back to your horses and you can leave peacefully.'

It had been ten years since Jonathon had last heard Lachlan speak, but despite the passage of time he recognized his voice.

'Lachlan,' he whispered to Troughton before both men swung round to face the boulder.

Only Lachlan's head was visible as he peered at them from behind his cover. He was far enough away that Jonathon wouldn't have recognized him if he hadn't have heard him speak, and so he guessed Lachlan might not be aware that he was confronting his stepbrother.

'Out here we're in no position to take control of this situation,' Troughton said from the corner of his mouth. 'So when I give the word run for cover.'

At the base of the slope there were numerous low-lying rocks that would give them cover, but they were also around seventy-five paces away over open ground.

'That's a big risk.'

'Then I suggest you run quickly.' Troughton smiled. 'And do it now.'

With that, Troughton set off for the slope, aiming for a spot close to the rock that resembled a bird. A moment later Jonathon followed him.

For around a dozen paces they pounded along without reprisal. Then Lachlan shouted a warning and when they continued to run he blasted lead.

The shots ripped into the dirt ahead of them and in response Troughton drew his gun and fired at the boulder. As he was running quickly the shots were wild, but one of them must have landed close to Lachlan as he ducked down and that encouraged both men to run even harder.

In short order they approached a rock at the base of the slope and so Troughton dived to the ground, rolled and came to a halt on his belly in a position where Lachlan wouldn't be able to see him. As Jonathon prepared to carry out the same manoeuvre, he glanced at the boulder, seeing Lachlan edge back into view.

Behind Lachlan was the rock that had resembled a man's face when seen in profile from the ledge. From this position Lachlan was standing before a pointed rock that provided the outline of a nose and the sight gave Jonathon the odd feeling that he'd had earlier.

He slid to a halt and looked the rock over, but then Lachlan fired at him and this time his shot was close enough for the lead to whistle by only feet to his side.

The gunshot broke him out of his reverie and he hurried on. Then he did the same as Troughton had done and rolled into cover to come to a halt lying beside the sheriff.

'Why did you stop out there?' Troughton said while directing a bemused expression at him.

Jonathon didn't reply immediately and looked up. He could no longer see Lachlan, but he could see most of the two rock formations that had concerned him.

Now, with him no longer in danger of being shot, he was able to identify why the rocks had made him feel odd.

'Because I've just realized something,' he said. 'I know this place.'

Troughton frowned. 'I thought you said that you've never been to Saddle Pass before.'

'I haven't.' Jonathon sighed. 'Despite that, this place is familiar, and that sure is mighty strange.'

CHAPTER 14

'Those are the men I saw outside Lerado,' Willoughby declared.

'You do have a talent for following men,' Devine said. 'Now show me your other talent and tell me what they're doing.'

Willoughby shrugged. 'I can't tell that yet, but I'll figure it out before long.'

'Do it. You have one hour.'

Devine shoved Willoughby on to stand at the far end of the boulder that they were using for cover. Then he settled down to await developments.

Willoughby had picked up the trail of the men who had been watching Lerado a few miles out of town and they had followed it north. Their trail was an obvious one, but Devine had given Willoughby enough leeway to make a mistake by letting him take the lead.

As it had turned out, Willoughby hadn't tried

any tricks and he had followed the trail to Hangman's Gulch, the scene of the gunfight twenty years ago where the raiders had made their last stand.

Devine was familiar with the area and so he and Willoughby had moved to higher ground and then climbed down to a spot within the gulch that was around a hundred feet up where they could look down on the men.

One man had been dispatched to the entrance to the gulch to keep lookout while the remaining four men had taken up positions on either side.

When an hour had passed without any developments, Willoughby sidled back to Devine.

'They're waiting for someone,' he said. 'I reckon they're planning to mount an ambush.'

'That's obvious.' Devine sneered. 'If I didn't want them to know we're here yet, I'd throw you down into the gulch for making that stupid comment.'

Willoughby looked around without much hope and then turned back to Devine.

'I can't offer nothing more than that I reckon they must be waiting for Sheriff Troughton and Jonathon Lynch.'

'Except those men didn't head this way, but we can't let them be disappointed.' Devine raised himself to loom over Willoughby. 'You'll ride up to the entrance and ask them what they're doing.'

100

Willoughby opened his eyes wide. 'If I do that, they'll probably shoot me up.'

'They won't. After all, you reckon they're waiting for the lawman and the bounty man.'

Willoughby gulped. 'I'm a bounty hunter.'

'I know. Now get down there and tell them how much you like collecting bounty.'

Devine glared at Willoughby until he started to turn away, but then he grabbed his arm and drew him back. 'Don't try anything.'

He held on to Willoughby until Willoughby lowered his head, and then pushed him on. When Willoughby had made his way back up the slope and out of the gulch, Devine settled down to see how the men would react.

Thirty minutes passed before the lookout man got his colleagues' attention. In a moment, with practiced efficiency, two men dropped down from view while two other men moved into prominent positions where they could watch the entrance.

Presently, Willoughby came into view. He was riding openly, albeit with his neck craned as he peered ahead cautiously.

When he rode through the entrance, he avoided looking towards the high point where the lookout man was hiding. Then he rode down the centre of the gulch until he saw the two standing men.

He hailed them with a wave and although they

didn't react, he still rode on. When he reached a spot below Devine that put him in the midst of the four men, one of them gestured at him to stop.

Willoughby drew to a halt and leaned forward in the saddle.

'Is this Hangman's Gulch?' he called, his voice clear to Devine in his elevated position.

'Sure,' one man said. 'What do you want?'

'I was looking for somewhere to rest up and I'd heard this gulch is a decent place.'

The two standing men glanced at each other after which the speaker moved closer to Willoughby.

From his position Devine was able to see that the two hidden men edged forward while taking advantage of the available cover to avoid Willoughby seeing them.

With everyone's attention being on Willoughby, Devine slipped out from behind the boulder. Placing his feet to the ground with care, he moved downwards towards the hidden man on his side of the gulch.

'You heard right,' the man called. 'Why should we let you stay?'

'I'm right friendly, I have plenty of supplies that I'll gladly share, and I'm unarmed.'

The last comment made the two men glance at each other again and even from some distance away Devine could see that they relaxed.

'In that case, join us.'

'I'm much obliged.'

Willoughby dismounted and moved towards the speaker while his companion hurried down to the bottom of the gulch to approach Willoughby from behind. His action made Willoughby look over his shoulder nervously and stop walking, and so the approaching man raised his hands.

'Don't worry,' that man said. 'We're all friends. What's your business out here?'

Willoughby sighed and lowered his voice so that Devine could barely hear him.

'I'm a bounty hunter.'

Both men straightened up and they edged their hands towards their holsters while the two hidden men swung their guns up so they could turn them on Willoughby the moment they were given the order to act.

'Name?'

'I'm Willoughby Jeffries.'

The standing men glanced at each other and then shrugged, but Devine had seen enough and he aimed at the hidden guntoter below him.

He blasted a shot, catching the fellow in the back and making him slump forward over his covering rock. Then he fired at the man who had been approaching Willoughby from behind.

This man was further away and Devine needed three shots to dispatch him. The gunfire echoed in the narrow gulch and that made it sound as if several men were involved in the ambush.

The two men on the other side of the gulch looked around frantically, seeking out where the shooting was coming from and so Devine dropped down behind a large rock.

He reloaded and when he peered over the top, the two survivors in the gulch had stopped looking for whoever was shooting at them and they were facing Willoughby with their guns raised.

For his part, Willoughby was scurrying to safety and he was heading towards Devine's side of the gulch.

Both gunmen blasted lead at Willoughby, but their shots were wild and they kicked grit to either side of him. Then Willoughby reached the end of the flat ground at the bottom of the gulch and he had no choice but to start climbing.

With Willoughby's progress becoming slow both men moved purposefully towards him. They stilled their fire until they were close enough to be sure of delivering accurate shots.

Willoughby glanced down and when he saw the advancing gunmen, he looked up. The slope above him became even steeper giving him little hope of putting a significant distance between himself and danger, so he sought cover nearby.

His change of direction encouraged the men to stop. Then they both fired again at Willoughby.

So, reckoning that they had come as close as they ever would, Devine hammered lead at the nearest gunman.

His first shot tore into the man's chest making him drop down to his knees and then fall over on to his side. Devine fired at the second man, but this man had worked out where his opponent was and he blasted a slug at him that sliced into the rock a foot below Devine's head.

Devine didn't duck down and he fired two rapid shots, the second of which winged the man's left arm making him twitch and stumble for a pace before he righted himself. With Devine having got the man in his sights, his next shot ploughed into the centre of the man's forehead making him topple over backwards.

Then Devine leapt to his feet and while reloading he clambered down into the gulch. Willoughby stood below him and he appeared unharmed as he considered the aftermath of the gunfight while nodding with approval.

He even swung round to smile at Devine as he approached, but the man he'd shot in the chest was now crawling away and so Devine ignored him. He stormed past Willoughby and hurried down the final stretch of slope.

When he reached the bottom the wounded man was still shuffling away, his progress leaving a trail of blood behind him.

'Stop!' Devine called.

The man flopped down, either because he was following the order or because his strength had given out. Then he pressed a hand to the ground and with a grunt of effort he levered himself over to lie on his back.

'Are you another bounty hunter?' he murmured.

Devine sneered. 'I'm US Marshal Jake T. Devine.'

Devine waited for that information to register and then blasted a slug between the man's eyes, making his head jerk back before he collapsed. Then Devine looked to the side.

Since the gunfight had started he hadn't seen the lookout man again and so he walked towards the entrance to the gulch. He kept his gaze on the last place he'd seen him while ensuring he could see either side of the gulch from the corners of his eyes.

He had covered a hundred paces when Willoughby called out from behind him.

'Look out, Devine!' he shouted.

Devine turned at the hip, seeing the lookout man stepping out from behind the cover of a grouping of boulders fifty feet up the side of the gulch, having presumably made his way closer stealthily during the gunfight.

The man had enough time to fire a shot that

whistled by Devine's head, but then Devine settled his stance and hammered lead into the man's right calf.

The man cried out and staggered an uncertain pace to the side. Then his leg gave out and he went tumbling down into the gulch, kicking up a trailing plume of dust.

He rolled for more than a dozen times before he slammed to a halt ten paces ahead of Devine, who paced forward to stand over him. Devine kicked his gun away and then looked him over, noting his battered form.

'Who are you?' he demanded.

The man tried to raise his head, but he failed and with a groan he slumped down on his back.

'Vincent Grout,' he murmured.

Devine nodded and then stomped a heavy boot down on Vincent's wounded leg. He waited until Vincent stopped screaming and then raised his boot.

'Why did you ambush a US Marshal?'

'We didn't know who you were,' Vincent said, his breath coming in harsh bursts. 'We thought you were bounty hunters.'

'The scum over there is. I'm not. Now talk.'

Before Vincent could summon the strength to reply, Devine slammed his boot down again, grinding his heel into Vincent's bloodied calf.

This time Vincent sat up and tried to bat

Devine's leg away, so Devine cuffed him about the head knocking him down again. He ground his heel in one more time and then stepped back.

'We were waiting for those bounty hunters from Lerado,' Vincent said through gritted teeth. 'We don't like manhunters.'

Devine chuckled. 'You make a good point. They're scum, but I wipe out scum, not you. Now, why are you shooting up the bounty men who come here?'

Devine raised his foot for emphasis, making Vincent look at it with frightened eyes. Then with his good leg he sought to shove himself away from Devine, but in his weak state he moved for only a few inches.

'We're not. We only attack the ones who attack us.'

Devine thought back. When Willoughby had ridden into the gulch and revealed that he was a bounty hunter, the men had got ready to attack him, but when he'd revealed his name, they had been less assured.

'That's a lie. You're looking for one particular bounty man.' Devine kicked Vincent's calf. 'Give me a name.'

'I can't,' Vincent said and then screeched in pain when Devine kicked him again.

Devine waited, but Vincent only repeated his refusal to answer, so he stepped back.

'That's all I wanted to hear,' he said.

Devine smiled. Then he raised his gun and fired, blasting Vincent in the face.

He stepped forward to stand over Vincent's body and spat on its ruined face. Then he turned away to find that Willoughby was sidling closer.

'Did you find out what they wanted?' he asked.

'They hate bounty men.' Devine licked his lips. 'I can't blame them for that.'

'You should.' Willoughby gestured at the spot up the slope where Vincent had fired at Devine. 'I saved your life.'

'You did.' Devine narrowed his eyes. 'A mistake?'

Willoughby set his hands on his hips with a defiant gesture, but then conceded Devine's assumption with a sigh.

'Yeah,' Willoughby said with his shoulders slumping. 'I called out a warning to you without thinking.'

'So you don't think.' Devine walked up to Willoughby and slapped his shoulder so hard the blow knocked him aside. 'I reckon I've found your third talent.'

CHAPTER 15

'Did you bang your head while you were up on the ledge?' Troughton said.

'I know I'm not making sense,' Jonathon said. 'All I can say is that I have a memory involving those two rock formations that look like a bird and a man's face, even though I've never been to this place before.'

Troughton shrugged. 'That would suggest you've seen similar rocks somewhere else.'

Jonathon shook his head. 'That's not it. The memory is vivid, and from a long time ago.'

The moment he said that the memory was an old one, he was able to recall why this place was familiar. The recollection made him groan and lower his head until he rested his forehead on the ground.

'What have you just worked out?'

'I reckon I know why Lachlan's here.'

When Jonathon sat up, Troughton considered him with an eyebrow raised, requesting an expla- nation, but Jonathon hadn't got his own thoughts in order yet and he looked aside. So Troughton got up on his haunches and considered the lie of the land.

'Can you use that reason to help us capture him?' he asked.

'I don't know. He did enough shooting to prove he won't listen to sense.'

Troughton sighed. 'Last night I asked you whether I could trust you if we found Lachlan and we ended up in a difficult situation. Well, we have found him and we are in a difficult situation.'

'I gave you my word. You can trust me.'

'In that case, pull yourself together and cover me.'

Troughton gave Jonathon a long look and then raised himself. Jonathon followed his lead in rising up, and that appeared to satisfy Troughton as he blasted two quick shots at Lachlan.

When Lachlan didn't return fire, Troughton vaulted on to the flat length of rock that they were using as cover and then sprinted for the nearest large rock formation.

When Jonathon raised his head until he could see the boulder, Lachlan had ducked down, so he kept his gun holstered and walked towards Lachlan's position. The boulder was around fifty

111

paces away and when he had covered the first ten paces, Lachlan still hadn't appeared while Troughton had nearly reached the rock.

Then Lachlan bobbed up. When he saw the approaching men, he snapped up his gun arm and sighted the running sheriff, but in response Jonathon only raised his arms.

'Don't shoot, Lachlan,' he called. 'It's your brother.'

'Jonathon?' Lachlan said.

He had sounded surprised, and thankfully that surprise was great enough for him not to fire, letting the sheriff reach the rock safely.

'Yeah,' Jonathon said as he continued walking towards Lachlan. 'I've come to work out what's been going on out here. Now that I've seen this place, I reckon I know why it interests you, too.'

'Of course you know, but you're here with Sheriff Troughton and that means you're trying to get rid of me so you can claim the gold for yourself.'

'I'm not here for the gold. I'm here to help you sort out the mess you're in.'

'Stay out of this. We're not exactly kin and if you don't back off, I will shoot you.'

From the corner of his eye Jonathon saw Troughton move out from the other side of the rock formation. Then he crawled along using a path that would let him reach the boulder without

Lachlan seeing him.

'I can't do that, Lachlan,' Jonathon said as he continued walking. 'We need to figure this out together and I reckon I might be the only one who can help you do that.'

'I know that, but I'm not letting you cheat me out of what's rightfully mine, again.'

'I've never cheated you before. I—' Jonathon broke off when Lachlan blasted a shot into the ground a foot from his right boot.

'That was your only warning. The next shot will be four feet higher.'

Jonathon stopped. Troughton was now twenty yards from the boulder and he must have been confident that Lachlan couldn't see him as he got to his feet and moved on, crouched over.

Jonathon judged that the sheriff would be in a position to take on Lachlan in less than a minute and so he spread his hands.

'I was going to say that I've never kept anything from you. It was only when I saw those two rocks that look like a bird and a man's face that I remembered the stories that Owen, your father, told us when we were children.' Jonathon shrugged. 'It was just about the only decent thing he ever did for me.'

Lachlan gestured at him. 'Don't speak ill of him again.'

'Then I won't. I liked his stories about a magical

land where the rocks were alive and how they helped people find their dreams. Except they weren't stories and he was describing this place, and that means Owen was once here. He was one of the men who found the gold.'

'You're not remembering it right. You're—' Lachlan would have said more, but then Troughton reached the boulder and without delay he charged behind it.

As Lachlan swirled round and then dropped down, Jonathon broke into a run. He saw brief glimpses of Lachlan and Troughton as they struggled, but then both men disappeared from view.

Jonathon pounded on and he rounded the boulder on the run to find Troughton and Lachlan were lying on the ground.

Both men were trying to turn Lachlan's gun on to their opponent making the gun swing wildly from side to side. So Jonathon wasted no time in rushing to them and grabbing Lachlan's wrist.

With Jonathon and Troughton combining forces, Jonathon was able to dash the gun from Lachlan's hand. Then he stood back and trained his gun down on Lachlan.

'As you just said to me,' he said, 'we're not exactly kin and that means I'll shoot you if you don't surrender.'

Lachlan made one last determined effort to shove Troughton aside, but when he failed to move him he slumped and glared up at him.

'It may look as if you've won again, Jonathon, but this isn't over yet,' he said.

Jonathon shook his head as Troughton dragged Lachlan to his feet and stood him up against the boulder to frisk him.

'You keep saying that I've wronged you before, but I don't know what you mean.'

Lachlan sneered, but he said nothing until Troughton had finished checking that he didn't have a concealed weapon on him. Then he faced Jonathon, while Jonathon returned his gaze placidly.

'Perhaps you don't,' Lachlan said in a calmer tone. 'When we were children you sure were stupid.'

'Then we have that in common.'

Lachlan snorted a laugh and then looked Jonathon up and down while rubbing his jaw.

'We have more than that in common.' Lachlan turned to Troughton. 'Perhaps I ought to tell Jonathon what he came here to find out, but it's for his ears only.'

'If you're confessing to something, I need to hear it,' Troughton said.

'It's not exactly a confession, and as the proof of what I have to say is the gold and I haven't found that yet, it won't help you none.'

For long moments Troughton looked Lachlan

115

in the eye. Then he sighed and turned to Jonathon.

'If what he tells you could endanger lives, I expect to hear about it or you'll be in as much trouble as Lachlan is.'

Jonathon nodded and so Troughton backed away up the slope. The sheriff kept his gun trained on Lachlan, but nobody spoke until he was no longer near enough to hear them.

'What do you want to tell me?' Jonathon asked, keeping his voice low.

'That your memory isn't as good as you think it is. My father did tell you those stories, but apparently your father, Maynard, told them to you first.'

'What are you saying?' Jonathon gasped.

'That my father was one of the original men who found the gold in this pass, and so was Maynard.'

Jonathon gulped. 'You're lying. My father was a decent man who always did right by his family.'

'All the men who found the gold were decent men, and they fell victim to men who were less decent. Maynard was in Hangman's Gulch, but he fled with the gold before the final battle, not that his treachery did him any good.'

Jonathon raised his hat to run fingers through his hair as he gathered his thoughts.

'Owen survived, so that would suggest he ran away from that final battle, too.'

'I don't know what he had to do to survive, but I

do know that unlike Maynard he didn't have the gold.'

'So what happened to it?'

'Maynard buried it and made a map of its location. Then he returned to his family to wait for everything to calm down. Except someone came looking for him. He ran to protect you and your mother.'

Jonathon winced, now piecing together the next part of the story.

'Owen wanted the map and when he found out that my father had been killed, he wooed my mother to get his hands on it.'

'Except he wasn't a well man. By the time he'd found out what had happened to the map he wasn't fit enough to do anything about it.' Lachlan smiled. 'So he told me.'

Jonathon looked aside as he connected this revelation to the other information he had gathered.

'My father stored the map in a safe place in Fairmount Town's bank.'

'Sure, and his instructions were that in the event of his death, when you were eighteen the map would be sent to you. Then you could dig up the gold and live a contented life.'

Jonathon raised his chin. 'I never received that map, but if I had I wouldn't have taken something that wasn't rightfully mine.'

Lachlan shook his head. 'You're so noble, but

you'd have reacted differently if you'd have seen the casket brimming with gold. Either way, I decided to claim the map before it could be sent to you.'

'You raided Fairmount Town's bank with Wayne Jackson?'

'I didn't get the chance. I had enough sense to know I needed help, but I was naïve and I didn't find the right men to help me. Wayne beat the details out of me and carried out the raid himself. When he died, I joined the group looking for the fleeing raiders. I found one of the men that nobody knew had been involved, Scorpio Blake.'

Jonathon sneered. 'And you were so angry that you shot him.'

'I didn't. Scorpio had been entrusted with the map because he couldn't read. It had two parts with one half depicting a location and the other half having written instructions on how to get from that location to the gold. Both parts were useless on their own, so we agreed a deal where I'd have the written half and he'd have the diagram.'

'Then you shot him up for his half?'

Lachlan gestured angrily at him. 'You're not listening to me. Someone else shot Scorpio. Then that man stole his half of the map and framed me for the shooting.'

Jonathon sighed. 'I guess as the lawman can't hear you, you have no reason to lie about that.'

'I don't. When I came out of jail I found Scorpio and told him the truth. He believed me and so we looked for the gold again.'

'Scorpio will never find it now. He got killed a few days ago.'

Lachlan winced. 'That's unfortunate. I guess someone worked out that he raided the bank.'

'While telling everyone you did it.'

Lachlan shrugged. 'Perhaps he wasn't entirely convinced that I didn't shoot him.'

'I note you only told me that after I'd told you he was dead. I assume you'll also tell me that Scorpio killed the manhunters who came looking for you.'

'I didn't know that anyone was after me, but then again I don't know what Scorpio did when he wasn't here searching with me.'

Jonathon gestured at Lachlan's jacket. 'So you still have your half of the map?'

'I destroyed it.' Lachlan tapped his forehead. 'Now it's in here.'

'And the man who really shot Scorpio eight years ago has the other half?'

'I assume so, except it won't help him as he'll only know the starting point for the search, not what he has to do next.'

Jonathon snorted a rueful laugh. 'While you know what to do, but you don't know where to start.'

119

Lachlan spread his hands. 'Which brings us back to the stories you remember from childhood about a magical land with rocks shaped like a bird and a man's face. I reckon those stories described this place.'

'This is the place where they found the gold.' Jonathon shrugged. 'It's unlikely that my father buried it here.'

'Perhaps not, but without the other half of the map, where else can I start looking?'

Jonathon didn't have an answer to that and so with Lachlan's story told, he gestured for Troughton to return.

When the sheriff joined them, Troughton kept his gun on Lachlan and treated Jonathon to a stern look.

'I don't need to hear everything that you've just talked about,' he said. 'I only need to know about any crimes he's involved in.'

Jonathon lowered his head as he thought back through the events Lachlan had described. Then he looked up and faced Troughton.

'In the end he might not have committed any crimes. He claims that while he's been here searching for the gold, Scorpio raided the bank and then killed the manhunters that came looking for him.'

Lachlan nodded approvingly at Jonathon's short version of his story that avoided many of the details that were embarrassing for both of them, but

Troughton still looked sceptical.

'You expect me to believe that's all I need to know?'

Jonathon frowned as he again searched for an admittance of wrongdoing, but then something that he'd not thought about when Lachlan had mentioned it came back to him. He put a hand to his forehead as the full implications hit him, before with a shake of the head he got himself under control.

'There is one other matter,' he said. 'If Lachlan is telling the truth, twenty years ago someone came looking for my father and then killed him. That man would have been Marshal Devine.'

CHAPTER 16

'Get back here,' Devine demanded when Willoughby turned his horse away.

Willoughby swung back to face Devine. He gestured at Lerado, now a half-mile ahead, and then at the higher ground to the side.

'We've finished our mission,' he said. 'So I'm heading back to the rise where you found me.'

Devine pointed at the town. 'You're staying with me.'

'But you have to let me go. I saved your life back in the gulch. That has to count for something.'

'It did. I saved your life.'

'You didn't! You nearly killed me on the rise and then you could have got me killed when you sent me into the gulch unarmed.'

'You're alive. Quit whining.'

Devine glared at Willoughby until he conceded his demand with a reluctant nod. Then, at a steady trot, they rode towards town.

From a distance the town displayed no obvious signs of life, but Devine still directed Willoughby to slow down. When they reached the main drag, Cameron Morgan came into view at the opposite end of town.

He was standing in what had once been the doorway to the bank and he was peering straight ahead. He must have been engrossed with whatever he was looking at as he didn't register that Devine and Willoughby had arrived until they reached the centre of town.

Cameron swirled round to face them over a low and crumbling wall and then ducked down from view.

'He doesn't look as if he was expecting company,' Willoughby said.

'I can't see anyone being pleased to see you riding into town. Go on ahead and make sure your old friend is feeling peaceable.'

'He's unlikely to be pleased.' Willoughby rubbed his forehead. 'And how do you know that I know Cameron?'

'Bounty men are all friends.'

Willoughby tipped back his hat while shaking his head.

'Not in my experience,' he said, but he did as he'd been told and dismounted.

Then, one cautious pace at a time, he moved on

to the bank with his neck craned as he looked out for Cameron. When he reached a low stretch of wall, he raised a hand in greeting.

Cameron spoke up from inside the bank and so Willoughby swung round to nod to Devine. Then he clambered over a low length of wall.

Devine wasted no time in jumping down from his horse. He followed Willoughby to the bank, but he moved to the side and climbed over a heap of debris to come in through the doorway.

Inside, Cameron and Willoughby were eyeing each other with strained good humour. When Cameron saw Devine he set his feet wide apart, while Willoughby shuffled aside to let them face each other.

'You stayed,' Devine said.

'You told me to,' Cameron said with a shrug.

Devine stalked into the bank and placed his hands on his hips.

'The others left, but you'll do no better than they will.'

'I don't care what you think, Marshal.'

'That's not being friendly after I saved your life.' Devine glanced at Willoughby. 'You're as ungrateful as this bounty man.'

'How have you saved our lives?' Cameron asked.

'That's what I want to know,' Willoughby said and then gulped and lowered his head.

'It's no wonder you're so far behind the

outlaws,' Devine muttered. He paced across the bank, grabbed Willoughby's arm, and threw him towards Cameron. 'Tell him what we did in Hangman's Gulch.'

Willoughby came to a halt in front of Cameron and then swung round to face Devine, his face alighting with understanding.

'The men in the gulch have been shooting up the bounty hunters who came here to search for Lachlan.' Willoughby rubbed his jaw. 'That means it wasn't Lachlan who's been behind all this.'

Devine smiled. 'You got there in the end.'

Willoughby nodded and then turned back to Cameron.

'Before Sheriff Troughton and Jonathon Lynch left town, five men were watching Lerado. When those men left, we followed them to Hangman's Gulch. They must have been expecting that some of you would go there and they planned to mount an ambush, except Devine got to them first.'

Cameron digested this information while nodding.

'So those men have been waiting for bounty hunters to follow the clues to Hangman's Gulch and then they killed them.' Cameron sighed. 'That sure is sneaky.'

'I can understand why anyone would want to kill bounty men,' Devine said. 'But they weren't ambushing everyone who came along. They were waiting for one particular bounty man to come looking for Lachlan.'

'That sure is interesting,' Cameron said with a shrug. 'And where is Lachlan?'

'As I told you before, Lachlan will come to Lerado.' Devine grinned. 'So we wait.'

CHAPTER 17

'If you ever find the gold, you won't be able to keep it,' Troughton said when the group settled down that night.

'You'll have to prise it out of my dead hands,' Lachlan said, peering at Troughton over their campfire. 'Just like Maynard did to the others.'

Jonathon felt unwilling to be drawn into another debate with Lachlan and so he lowered his head. His thoughts were still dwelling on the fact that twenty years ago Devine had been tasked with rounding up the men who had escaped from Hangman's Gulch, and his father had been one of those men.

He had never been told how his father had died beyond the fact that he wasn't at home at the time, and that could mean that his mother had kept from him the fact that his demise had been a violent one.

With him brooding about the past throughout the day as Troughton had escorted Lachlan back along the pass, he had been quiet, as had the other two men. At sundown they had made camp in the entrance to the pass.

Lachlan hadn't given them any trouble, but then again, if his story was to be believed, he hadn't committed any crimes and he hadn't even been guilty of the one crime for which he had been convicted.

'Be assured that it'll end that way for you,' Troughton said. 'So if I can prove your innocence, I suggest you seek out a life that has a more promising future.'

'What future can be better than the one the gold can give me?'

Troughton sighed. 'Jonathon's kept his word and not told me what you said to him beyond the fact that since leaving jail you've done nothing wrong. I'm inclined to believe that, and if you cooperate it's likely that I'll be able to prove that Scorpio Blake raided Fairmount Town's bank, but that still leaves the question of the bounty.'

'What bounty?'

'The four-thousand-dollar bounty on your head that all those dead manhunters were trying to claim.'

Lachlan opened his mouth and then closed it, his shock at this revelation appearing genuine.

'I didn't know about that,' he said after a while. 'Someone must think I know more about the gold's location than I do.'

'That seems likely. It'll take us another two days to return to Fairmount Town. I suggest you use that time to work out who posted that bounty or you might not get the chance to look for the gold again.'

Lachlan gave a worried nod and with that they settled down for the night.

The next day they set off before first light and rode at a steady mile-eating pace. Troughton directed them along the same route that they had used to reach Saddle Pass and that meant they would ride through Lerado again.

As the town was a convenient place to stop for the night, Jonathon didn't suggest they take a different route, but it meant that they would probably meet Cameron again.

He still didn't know what had made Cameron have a change of heart about their partnership, but with his thoughts still dwelling on Devine he wasn't concerned about meeting him again.

It was approaching sundown when they first saw Lerado ahead. Troughton directed them to slow down and then pointed at a weak haze over the town.

Jonathon peered at the haze until he identified it as being smoke rising up from the mission and which with the lack of wind, was lazily spreading out over the town.

'So Cameron's still here waiting for Lachlan to ride into town,' Jonathon said.

'Then I hope he won't be disappointed that we found him first,' Troughton said before directing them to move on cautiously.

They stopped outside the bank and as the only sign of life was the rising smoke, they dismounted. Troughton took the lead in heading to the mission with Lachlan and Jonathon walking together behind him.

When they reached the door Troughton stood to one side while listening, but Cameron spoke up from inside.

'Come in,' he said. 'We were expecting company.'

Troughton directed a shrug at the other two men and then moved into the doorway. He uttered a murmur of surprise before he headed inside and so Jonathon followed him with Lachlan at his heels.

When he saw who was with Cameron, he couldn't help but utter a grunt of surprise, too.

Willoughby Jeffries was sitting by the fire with Cameron while beyond the fire in the position he had adopted when they'd last been here was

Marshal Devine.

'So we're all here now,' Devine said with a harsh grin. 'That means we can begin.'

CHAPTER 18

'You're not starting anything, Devine,' Troughton said. 'I've arrested Lachlan and so now this is over.'

'So you think that stumbling across Lachlan ends it, do you, lawman?' Devine said.

Troughton spread his hands. 'There's still the matter of the missing gold, but it's been missing for twenty years and right now I don't care about it.'

'Neither do I, but that's not what this is about.' Devine looked around the group of men. 'Nobody leaves the mission.'

Troughton sighed. 'You made that demand before and yet you still left town. It doesn't hold much weight the second time.'

'Most of us left and we had ourselves some fun. Now we're back and this time everybody that needs to be here is here. We have Lachlan, Lachlan's brother, Jonathon's friend, the bounty man, the lawman and me. We don't need nobody else and nobody leaves until the end.'

'It's you that's wrong, Devine. Nobody leaves until sunup tomorrow.' Troughton smiled. 'Then I'm taking Lachlan back to Fairmount Town to finish my investigation.'

Devine didn't retort and so the newcomers moved on to take up positions around the fire.

Jonathon was unwilling to talk with Cameron now that their partnership had ended and so he sat apart from him and on the opposite side of the fire to Devine. Cameron eyed both him and Lachlan with interest and that appeared to encourage Lachlan to sit beside him.

For a while they were all silent, but presently Willoughby started chattering about nothing in particular and that encouraged Troughton and Cameron to talk. Then Lachlan shuffled closer to Jonathon and leaned his head towards him.

'Is Devine the man you talked about in Saddle Pass?' he whispered.

'Yeah,' Jonathon whispered. 'The marshal was tasked with rounding up the men who escaped from Hangman's Gulch. I'd guess Owen McKinley was one of the few men who escaped his justice.'

'Not that it did him any good. He was so desperate to avoid being found that he had to marry your mother.'

Jonathon snorted a laugh. 'And I hope she

made his final years miserable.'

Lachlan laughed, but then directed a serious look at Jonathon.

'Why is Devine insisting that we can't leave?'

'It's the way he works,' Jonathon said. He raised his voice to a normal speaking volume. 'He pushes people until they break, and he reckons that demand will force us into doing something we don't want to do or into revealing something we want to keep secret.'

Lachlan glanced around as the chatter around the fire petered out and everyone looked at them, but he replied using a normal speaking volume.

'Forcing us to stay here won't change anything. I don't know where the gold is and anyhow, Devine said he doesn't care about it.'

Jonathon nodded and then turned to consider Devine through the flames.

'So what do you want, Devine?' he asked.

'What I always want,' Devine said. 'To finish the job I started and wipe out all the scum.'

Jonathon shrugged. 'Aside from the sheriff, none of us are exactly angels, but then again none of us have done anything that should concern a US Marshal either.'

Devine sneered. 'You will.'

'That's only because you reckon you can provoke an argument by demanding that we stay in the mission.'

Devine glanced at the door. 'Then try to leave and see what happens.'

Jonathon was minded to do just that and set in motion the confrontation Devine wanted, but to his surprise Cameron spoke up.

'You're right that Devine has a plan, Jonathon,' he said, 'but don't make it easy for him to complete it.'

'I'm pleased that you care about my welfare,' Jonathon said, 'but I'll do what I deem is necessary.'

'Then do it, but don't act before you know all the facts. What Devine hasn't mentioned is that he and Willoughby headed to Hangman's Gulch. They were ambushed by five men who were laying in wait for them.'

Jonathon flinched with surprise and then glanced at Lachlan, who looked at him with wide eyes that registered his shock.

'I didn't know that,' Lachlan said. He looked aloft as he considered. 'Scorpio recruited hired guns for protection and it must have been those men who launched the ambush. I guess that while I looked for the gold, they tasked themselves with fighting off anyone who tried to stop me finding it.'

Jonathon shook his head in disbelief and so Lachlan turned to Troughton, who considered him with an equal level of disbelief.

'I've tried to keep an open mind about you,' Troughton said. 'I was prepared to accept your story that you didn't know that Scorpio was shooting up manhunters, but you knew that he hired guns and that changes everything.'

'I didn't know what Scorpio and those men were doing and I sure didn't know they were ambushing men in the gulch.'

Troughton shook his head, but when he didn't reply, Cameron spoke up.

'They didn't ambush all the men who went here,' he said. 'They ambushed only the bounty hunters who came looking for you.'

Lachlan tipped back his hat and glanced around a group in which everyone was looking equally surprised. Then he looked into the flames.

'The four-thousand-dollar bounty on my head attracted bounty hunters,' he mused. 'Then Scorpio and his hired guns killed them. That would suggest it wasn't so much a bounty as a trap to lure manhunters here, and that means Scorpio must have posted that bounty.'

'It's an interesting theory,' Troughton said. 'But how would Scorpio get his hands on that much money?'

'The four thousand dollars stolen in the bank raid eight years ago was never found. Scorpio must have ended up with it.'

'It's possible, but for you to be right about this,

Scorpio sure must have had a deep hatred for bounty hunters.'

'And for me,' Lachlan said. 'He used me as the bait.'

'Maybe, but I'll still take some convincing that you didn't know about this.' Troughton glanced at Devine. 'I'd guess that's the question on Devine's mind that he wants to answer here today.'

Lachlan gulped and looked at Devine, but the marshal didn't return his gaze and instead he looked at Cameron.

'Tell him the rest, Jonathon's friend,' Devine said.

Cameron considered Devine before he turned to Troughton.

'Devine reckons that Scorpio didn't just lay a trap for all bounty hunters,' he said. 'He wanted to attract one particular man.'

'Who?' Troughton said.

Cameron shrugged and then looked around for someone else to make a comment, but only Jonathon met his eye.

'I've already told you, lawman,' Devine said. 'Everybody that needs to be here is here. We have Lachlan, Lachlan's brother, Jonathon's friend, the bounty man, the lawman and me. One of those men knows more than he's let on, and so nobody leaves until that man bites the dirt.'

'There are only three bounty hunters here,'

Jonathon said, still looking at Cameron. 'I know that Scorpio couldn't have had a problem with me, and Willoughby's too stupid for anyone to go to all this trouble to attract him. That leaves you.'

While Willoughby muttered to himself, Cameron shook his head.

'That's one way of looking at it,' Cameron said. 'Except I know that Scorpio wouldn't want to kill me, and Willoughby is so stupid it's a surprise he's got this far. That leaves you.'

Jonathon smiled. 'So there's me reckoning you're the man Scorpio wanted while you're claiming it was me. We both can't be right.'

Cameron raised himself slightly, his movement letting him edge his hand towards his holster.

'We can't. So how are we going to sort this out?'

Jonathon settled his weight to the side to ensure he could reach his holster quickly.

'I reckon we should try to answer one simple question: why would Scorpio want to entice one particular bounty hunter here?'

Cameron smiled. 'You're Lachlan's stepbrother and you and he don't exactly enjoy each other's company.'

'You're right, but it looks as if Scorpio was behind all this, not Lachlan. So why would Scorpio, a man who was helping Lachlan find the gold, want to get you here?'

Cameron didn't reply as he inched his hand

closer to his gun. Jonathon matched his movement, but then Lachlan murmured an oath under his breath.

'It was you all along,' he said, glaring at Cameron. 'You were the man who shot Scorpio eight years ago. Then you stole his half of the map and framed me for the shooting. Scorpio figured that out and—'

Lachlan didn't get to complete his accusation as Cameron whirled his hand to his gun. His gun had yet to clear leather when a gunshot thundered and a moment later Cameron went tumbling down to lie on his chest.

Jonathon still drew his gun, but he kept it lowered when he saw the blood spilling out from under Cameron's form. Cameron failed to move again, and so he looked past his body at Devine, who had already turned his smoking gun on him.

'Slow reactions, Lachlan's brother,' Devine said. 'I don't want to make a habit of saving the lives of bounty men.'

'You don't know nothing about saving lives,' Jonathon muttered. 'You only take them.'

Devine shrugged, but he kept his gun aimed until Jonathon holstered his weapon. Then he lowered his Peacemaker.

For long moments Lachlan stared at the scene with horror before he shuffled along to Cameron's body. He turned the body on to its back before with feverish movements he riffled through its pockets.

'All these years I've wanted to find the man who stole the other half of the map,' he said as he searched. 'Then Cameron gets killed just before I can find out the truth.'

'The map is probably in his saddlebag,' Jonathon said. He glanced at the door. 'On the way in I reckon I saw a horse in the old bank.'

Lachlan ripped his hand from Cameron's final pocket and then stood back from the body.

'I doubt it. Cameron was no fool. He probably did what I did and memorized the location where you have to start searching for the gold.'

Despite his comment, Lachlan still stood up and took a pace towards the door making Devine grunt a warning and aim his gun at Lachlan's back.

'Our horses *are* in the bank,' Devine said when Lachlan stomped to a halt. 'But as I keep on telling you all: nobody leaves the mission.'

CHAPTER 19

'I'm not trying to leave the town,' Lachlan said. 'I just want to leave the mission.'

Devine stood up and set his feet wide apart.

'Try it,' he muttered.

Lachlan's eyes were still feverish and Jonathon thought for a moment that he might run for the door, but then Troughton spoke up.

'I assume this map you want shows the location of the missing gold,' he said.

Lachlan winced and his shoulders slumped as he appeared to come to his senses and accept that he'd revealed more of his plans than he'd intended to.

'It is,' he said.

'Then you're going nowhere.'

Lachlan glanced at the door while rocking his weight on to his toes. Jonathon raised a warning hand.

'Start thinking sensibly, Lachlan,' Jonathon said. 'Listen to the sheriff.'

'That's easy for you to say. You haven't spent all your life dreaming about getting the gold only to see the chance stolen away.'

'Your search doesn't have to end here. You think you know where to start looking and only you know the second half of the instructions.'

'I only know the general area, and those instructions don't amount to much either.' Lachlan looked at each man in turn and then shrugged. 'I just have to face in a particular direction, walk thirty paces and then make two turns taking ninety-five paces each time.'

Jonathon narrowed his eyes. 'I doubt that's the real instruction you memorized from your half of the map.'

Lachlan raised his hat to run fingers through his hair, while sporting a weary expression that spoke of the long months he'd spent searching without luck.

'It is,' he said. 'The final part of those instructions is that when you reach the right spot, you have to dig down fifteen feet. It takes an age to do that and if you're in the wrong place by even a few paces, you'll only dig up dirt. So what use is knowing those directions if you don't have the exact starting point?'

'I can see that. So stop thinking about the gold

and start helping Sheriff Troughton prove you didn't raid Fairmount Town's bank and that you weren't involved in shooting up the bounty hunters.'

Lachlan kicked at the dirt on the floor and then with a sigh he sat down beside Cameron's body. With him calming down, Troughton nodded approvingly.

'Now that this is over, I'll check out Cameron's saddlebag,' he said. 'Then you're going to do what Jonathon said and tell me everything you know.'

Troughton looked at Lachlan. When Lachlan didn't respond, Troughton turned to the door, but the moment he took a pace, Devine swung his gun away from Lachlan to aim it at the sheriff's back.

'Nobody leaves the mission,' he said.

Troughton straightened up, but he didn't turn around.

'No lawman gives orders to another lawman,' he said calmly. 'I know you're trying to put everyone on edge to see what happens, but this is over now. Cameron all but confessed and once I've checked out everything, the situation will become clear.'

'That's why some lawmen give orders to other lawmen.'

Troughton raised his head to glance at the sky through the roof and then took a slow pace towards the door. He waited for a moment, but when Devine didn't react he continued walking.

Jonathon watched Devine, as did Willoughby, but Lachlan kept his head lowered, now looking as if he wanted to stay out of the argument.

Jonathon still couldn't believe that Devine would go through with his threat, but nothing in Devine's resolute gaze and firm gun hand suggested that he wouldn't fire if Troughton tried to go through the door.

'Troughton's right, Devine,' Jonathon said when the sheriff was five paces from the door. 'This is over now.'

'I don't care what Lachlan's brother says,' Devine said.

'You will care.' Jonathon rolled his shoulders. 'If you shoot the sheriff, I'll kill you.'

'Tough words, but if you lay a hand on your gun, you'll die.'

Troughton was still walking slowly to the door and in a matter of moments he'd be able to slip outside.

'You can't kill both of us.' Jonathon moved his hand towards his holster. 'Let Troughton leave and find out about this map.'

Devine said nothing while Troughton continued walking until he reached the doorway, where he stopped. He turned around to face Devine and raised an eyebrow.

'So you have turned a gun on me,' he said. 'I've heard plenty of bad things about you, but

144

even I didn't think you'd aim a gun at a fellow lawman. Lower your gun and then I'll check out the bank.'

'You don't give me orders,' Devine said. 'I give the orders and nobody leaves the mission.'

Troughton started to shake his head, but then he flinched and looked to the side. Jonathon followed his gaze to see that Lachlan now had a gun in his hand and with a snap of the wrist he raised it to aim the weapon over Cameron's body at Devine.

Cameron's body was lying with a posture that was more hunched than it had been before showing that while Troughton and Devine's argument had distracted everyone, Lachlan had claimed Cameron's gun.

'You just made a big mistake, Lachlan,' Devine said, although he didn't move his gun away from Troughton. 'Nobody threatens me and lives.'

'I'm not doing nothing other than leaving the mission to check out Cameron's saddlebag,' Lachlan said. 'Don't nobody try to stop me.'

Lachlan got to his feet. When he took a sideways step towards the door, Jonathon gestured at the floor signifying that he should stay.

'Don't do this, Lachlan,' he said. 'If you leave, it'll just make you look guilty of everything that's gone on around here, and Devine will kill you.'

'I spent seven years in jail because I got blamed

for what Cameron did to Scorpio,' Lachlan said while still moving on. 'If it gives me a chance to get to the gold, I'm prepared to get blamed for something else I didn't do.'

'The map might not be out there. Don't get yourself killed over nothing.'

Lachlan shook his head. While keeping his gun on Devine, he took one steady pace at a time until he reached the doorway where he stopped to consider everyone.

'Nobody leaves the mission,' he said.

With a swift motion, he ducked past Troughton. Then he leapt to the side to disappear from view.

A moment later Devine was storming across the mission and so Jonathon broke into a run.

He reached the doorway a few paces ahead of Devine and risked glancing outside. Lachlan was hurrying towards the bank with his head down.

He moved to follow him, but Devine slapped a hand on his shoulder and hurled him backwards so strongly, his feet left the floor before he slammed down on his back. He shook himself and then sat up as Devine darted through the doorway.

A moment later a gunshot blasted, followed by a second shot.

Jonathon winced and got to his feet. When he reached the doorway again, Troughton stood at his side and directed a warning shake of the head at him.

'Stay out of this and let the law deal with Lachlan,' he said.

'I'll let you deal with this,' Jonathon said.

Troughton nodded and then hurried through the door. Jonathon heard nothing other than Troughton's rapid footfalls and so with a heavy heart, he stepped through the doorway.

To his relief he couldn't see Lachlan, and so he assumed he must have reached the bank without getting shot. Devine was stalking down the main drag with his gaze set on a low stretch of wall while Troughton was hurrying along so that he could approach the bank from the side.

Despite the sheriff's order, Jonathon followed them at a run. He was twenty yards from the bank and slightly behind Devine when he stopped, and so Jonathon came to a halt, too.

Troughton continued to advance, but with the bank wall being almost complete at the corner, he would have to move further before he reached an area where the wall had collapsed so that he could see inside.

Jonathon did as Devine was doing and peered into the part of the building's interior that he could see, but as this area didn't include the horses, he could only be patient and wait for Lachlan to betray his position.

Then rapid gunfire blasted out from the bank making Troughton go on to one knee and

Jonathon glance around nervously. Devine didn't move.

Five shots sounded. Then silence reigned.

Troughton directed a bemused look in their direction and in return Jonathon shrugged. Then Troughton resumed walking and he covered another three paces before he came to a halt.

'You don't want to do that, Lachlan,' he said.

'I don't want to harm you, Sheriff,' Lachlan said from within the bank. 'Raise your hands and back away.'

'You need to listen to what Jonathon was telling you in the mission. You stand a good chance of walking away from all the recent trouble without getting blamed for any of it. Holding a gun on a lawman won't help you.'

'I reckon I'll take my chances.'

Troughton raised his hands and so Jonathon moved forward. He had to walk to within five paces of the bank before he saw Lachlan, and sure enough he had aimed his gun at the sheriff through a gap in the wall.

'Did you find the map, Lachlan?' he called.

Lachlan half-turned to him, ensuring he could still keep his gun on Troughton.

'I sure did,' he said. 'Cameron kept his half and so I now know where the gold is. I'm going to be a rich man.'

'You're going to be a dead man,' Devine said.

Jonathon turned to find Devine stalking closer and so he raised a hand.

'Stay out of this, Devine,' he said. 'You're not killing another member of my family.'

Devine stomped to a halt and looked him over.

'What are you talking about?'

'Twenty years ago you rounded up the men who had escaped from Hangman's Gulch. My father, Maynard Lynch, was one of those men, and he died.'

'Don't remember him.'

'I'm not surprised. You must have killed so many men you can no longer remember all their names.'

'I remember them all and I remember the look on their faces when I sent them to hell.' Devine glanced aloft as he thought back. 'I tracked down three men from the gulch and none of them was Maynard Lynch.'

'How can I believe you?'

'Believe me. I'm a lawman.' Devine sneered. 'If I'd have known your father was involved, I'd have killed him and then enjoyed telling you about his last moments.'

Jonathon gulped and then looked towards the bank.

'Then who did kill him?'

Even as he said the words the answer came to him, while in the bank Lachlan shuffled from foot to foot showing he'd heard their conversation and that he had just reached the same conclusion that Jonathon had.

'I don't know whether my father did it,' Lachlan called.

'Except you suspect he did,' Jonathon said. 'My father left us and died, and then later your father arrived. The obvious explanation is that Owen McKinley tracked down Maynard Lynch for the map and when he failed to get it, he killed him.'

Lachlan frowned, appearing lost for words, but then he tensed up while looking past Jonathon's right shoulder. Jonathon glanced that way to find that Devine had moved into Lachlan's line of sight and he'd aimed his gun at him.

'Time to die, scum,' he said.

'You won't shoot me,' Lachlan said. 'I've got something you all want. You heard the gunfire. I shot holes in the map and destroyed it. Now I'm the only man who knows the full story of where you start looking for the gold and where you then go.'

Devine took steady paces forward until he stood beside Jonathon.

'That sort of knowledge is dangerous.'

Lachlan raised a hand to wipe the sweat from his brow. He glanced at Troughton and then at Devine as he weighed up what his next move should be.

With a nod he appeared to reach a decision and

then beckoned for Troughton to come closer.

'I'm not backing down and I am getting my hands on the gold,' he said. 'So the sheriff and me are going to ride out of town. Nobody will follow us.'

Troughton set his feet wide apart and shook his head.

'I'm not going nowhere with you, Lachlan,' he said.

Devine chuckled and raised his gun hand a mite.

'Listen to the lawman,' he said.

'The lawmen aren't in charge here,' Lachlan said, his voice rising. 'I am. Without me, the gold will remain missing forever.'

Lachlan stabbed a finger against his chest and then beckoned with his gun for Troughton to approach, but that movement proved to be a mistake as it gave Devine an opening.

Devine fired and his shot tore into Lachlan's forehead, making him topple over backwards like a felled tree.

'Forever it is,' Devine said before he snapped round and turned his gun on Jonathon, who backed away for a pace.

'I accept he gave you no choice but to do that,' Jonathon said while raising his hands.

'I don't care what you accept. Now talk.'

Jonathon considered and then nodded when he

figured out what Devine had meant.

'I only had Lachlan's word that my father was involved in the Lerado bank raid. I know nothing about those events other than what he told us all and I care about the gold even less than you do.'

'That's not much of a reason for me not to blast you away.'

Devine directed a long look at him. When Jonathon didn't respond, he lowered his gun and moved on to face the advancing Troughton, who stopped before him and gestured angrily at the bank.

'Jonathon was right that you had to take that chance to kill Lachlan, but a better lawman would have found a way to talk him down.'

'Such as you?'

Troughton settled his stance and then raised his chin.

'Yeah.'

'Then be pleased I'm not as good a lawman as you are. Dead sheriffs are no use to anyone.'

Devine turned away to head to the bank, but Troughton moved round to stand before him.

'And dead outlaws who have useful information are no use to anyone either. You've just ensured that the gold stays missing, and that means it'll continue to attract trouble. Men will come looking for it and just like this time, those men will kill to get their hands on it.'

'Then you'd better hope that a good lawman is around to deal with the trouble.'

'Quit with the sarcasm, Devine, and just tell me why you let the truth die with Lachlan.'

Devine looked Troughton up and down and then spat on the ground.

'Because it's easy to be a saint in paradise.'

With that, Devine moved on towards the bank, leaving Troughton and Jonathon standing together.

'What was that supposed to mean?' Jonathon asked.

'I don't know, but that man knows nothing about saints,' Troughton said.

Jonathon nodded. 'He doesn't, but he sure finds it easy to be a devil in hell.'

CHAPTER 20

By the time Willoughby joined Jonathon and Troughton on the main drag, Devine had mounted up in the bank. Then Devine rode on.

Devine paused to cast a sneering glance at Lachlan's body and then rode through the collapsed length of wall. When he reached them, Troughton stood before his horse making Devine stop.

'Even if I don't approve of your methods, I understand what you did in the mission,' Troughton said. 'You kept pushing until somebody broke.'

Devine looked at Troughton. 'Now that this is over, I hope you learned something, lawman.'

'I didn't, but this isn't over until you answer one question: what would you have done if Lachlan hadn't claimed Cameron's gun and I'd have tried to leave the mission?'

Devine licked his lips and then with a shake of the reins he moved his horse past Troughton. As he rode by the mission, he started whistling.

The three men stood together to watch him leave.

'Devine didn't reply because he didn't have an answer,' Jonathon said. 'He failed to find the gold again and he couldn't admit that.'

'He didn't fail,' Troughton said. 'He did what he set out to do.'

'Then he should have set out to do more than just kill everyone who stood in his way. Then he could be a better lawman like you are.'

'I'm obliged for your support, but don't let Devine hear you speaking like that.' Troughton smiled and when Jonathon laughed, he pointed out of town. 'I've had enough of Lerado. It's still light enough to get a couple of hours closer to Fairmount Town tonight.'

'I agree,' Jonathon said and when Troughton moved on towards the bank, he turned to Willoughby. 'You're welcome to ride with us.'

'I ride alone,' Willoughby said.

'I know that, and I also know that after all this talk of buried gold you've decided to stay here for a while.'

'I thought I would.' Willoughby chuckled. 'I reckon I might be able to figure out where it is.'

'Nobody's found the place where it was buried

155

in the last twenty years. What makes you think you'll succeed?'

Willoughby shrugged. 'I don't, but then again, when word gets out about what's just happened, more men are sure to come here and one of them might have a good idea.'

Jonathon sighed. 'And you'll do what you always do and follow that man, and then steal his good idea?'

'Sure,' Willoughby said without concern and then moved to turn away, but Jonathon raised a hand.

'Just remember that your method led to you spending time with Marshal Devine. If you don't want that to happen again, now might be the time to change your method.'

Willoughby shrugged. 'I see no reason to change anything. I'm a bounty hunter, like you, and I hunt.'

Willoughby winked. Then he moved on to the bank.

Jonathon sighed and then turned to find that Troughton had dragged Lachlan's body outside and he was now heading to the mission, presumably to collect Cameron's body.

After Cameron's treachery, Jonathon was minded to leave him to complete the task alone and so he looked aside. That let him see Willoughby skulking along as he searched for a way into the bank, while in the other direction Devine was riding away.

'Troughton's not a lawman like Devine and I'm not a bounty hunter like Willoughby,' he said to himself.

Then he followed Troughton into the mission.

Four hours after Willoughby left Lerado, Devine rode back into town.

For the last three days Devine had watched Willoughby from up on the rise that Willoughby had used while he'd been awaiting developments.

Willoughby had stayed on after Jonathon and the sheriff had left and he had skulked through the buildings without displaying any obvious plan. When he left town, he'd headed north.

Devine had followed him until he proved that Willoughby was heading to Hangman's Gulch. Then he turned back.

When Devine reached the ruined bank, he dismounted and paced around the building until he located the area where the door had once stood.

He clambered over several heaps of stones until he stood on a rock that marked the centre of the doorway. This was the spot where Cameron had been standing when he and Willoughby had returned to town, and Cameron had moved away the moment he'd seen that he had company.

The door would have faced east and the outer

walls of the bank protruded around the door ensuring that he couldn't go to the left or right. So the only direction that would let him walk for thirty paces was straight ahead.

With a nod to himself Devine took thirty paces forward. As he had to clamber over rocks, it was hard to keep a straight line and so he headed back to the bank.

He cleared away the rocks until he created a path that would let him complete thirty uninterrupted paces along the ground. He carried out this task twice and when both journeys led to him ending up in the same place, he turned to the right.

The husk of an old building was around fifty paces ahead and as it would block his way he turned around. He walked for ninety-five paces and then was faced with a choice.

The ruined wreck of a building was ten paces to his right while the mission was to his left. The mission was around seventy-five paces away and he faced the door while the other building had no obvious entrance.

So with a steady gait he walked towards the mission, only stopping briefly when he reached the doorway. He paced inside and completed the count of ninety-five paces, which took him just beyond the centre of the mission.

A thin smile cracked Devine's grim visage. He

was standing on the very spot where he had rested up during the two times he'd been here with Sheriff Troughton and the others.

He kicked away the dirt from the floor to find that he was standing in the centre of a flagstone. Devine judged that the stone was substantial enough to deter anyone from trying to lift it unless they had good cause.

Even better, it was one of a dozen such stones and there was nothing to set this one apart from the others.

Devine kicked dirt from side to side and then dragged the remnants of the fire they'd lit over the stone. He stood back to consider the effect he'd created and he reckoned that the area didn't look as if it had ever been disturbed.

'Until the next time,' he said to himself.

Then he turned away and left the mission.